The CRIMSON MASK

Airship 27 Productions

The Crimson Mask

The Crimson Mask Takes Over © 2013 Terrence P. McCauley
The Mystery Man © 2013 Gary Lovisi
The Blood of the Mob © 2013 C. William Russette
Carnival of Lost Souls © 2013 J. Walt Layne

Published by Airship 27 Productions
www.airship27.com
www.airship27hangar.com

Interior and cover illustrations © 2013 Andy Fish

Editor: Ron Fortier
Associate Editor: Ray Riethmeier
Production and design by Rob Davis
Promotion and marketing by Michael Vance

ISBN-13: 978-0615909639
ISBN-10: 0615909639

Printed in the United States of America

10 9 8 7 6 5 4 3 2 1

The CRIMSON MASK

Volume One
TABLE OF CONTENTS

The Crimson Mask Takes Over
by Terrence P. McCauley

"I don't want no trouble, mister," the robber said. "Just money. That's all."

"Just stay calm, friend," Doc Clarke said as he took a closer look at the sweating man pointing a revolver at his chest. Doc noticed his emaciated frame. His wild eyes. His filthy clothes damp with sweat. His gun hand twitching from the effort of holding the small revolver.

This man wasn't just a common thug. He was a dope fiend. As much a victim as he was a criminal. A victim of his own addiction to a terrible new mystery drug sweeping through the city's unfortunate addict population.

Doc had learned the art of manipulating his voice long ago and adopted a soothing, paternal tone. He wanted to talk the gun out of this poor man's hand if he could.

"You're not a bad man, friend. You're just sick is all. You need care and treatment and I can give you both. Why don't you just put the gun away and let me take a look at you? I'm sure we'll have you feeling better in no time if you'd just…"

But the junkie's yellow eyes went wild, hungry. "There's only one thing that'll make me feel good and you ain't got it. Nobody can make me feel as good as He can. He can do anything." He jerked the barrel of the pistol down at the cash register, then back up at Doc. "Open it, damn it! Open it now!"

Doc had wanted to talk the gun out of the junkie's hand, but he'd take it if he had to. He kept speaking in his paternal tone. "Money's the last thing you need right now, friend. You're too far along and won't last a week if you keep taking that poison." Doc pointed to the mirror behind the counter. "Take a good look at yourself. Your skin and eyes are yellow because your liver is diseased and beginning to shut down. You can't live without a liver." Doc could've listed half a dozen other things that were wrong with the man, but he cut to the chase. "You're dying. Right here and right now. If you'll just let me help you, I can …"

"Shut up!" the junkie screamed. "Just shut your filthy mouth! I didn't come in here for a damned lecture. I came in here for money and I want it. I want all of it right now!"

And that's when the red call light he'd installed under the counter began to blink and buzz quietly. The call light he'd installed whenever his patron, Commissioner Warrick called for the Crimson Mask.

Doc hoped the gunman hadn't seen the blinking light or heard the faint buzzing.

But he had.

"What's that?" The junkie's eyes went even wilder. "Is that an alarm? Did you call the cops? You did, didn't you?" Doc watched his hand quiver as he tried to thumb back the hammer on the pistol. "You ratted me out, didn't you, you ..."

In one fluid motion, and with a speed no pharmacist should have, Doc snatched the gun out of the man's hand and backhanded him with the butt of the pistol across the jaw.

The addict collapsed like a sack of wet leaves; unconscious before he even hit the floor.

Doc easily vaulted the counter and put two fingers to the man's thin neck, checking for a pulse. The skin was cold and gooseflesh, but Doc could feel a pulse. It was weak and erratic, but there. He was still alive. Barely.

Doc knew the blow to the jaw hadn't done that to him. Whatever drugs the man had been pumping into his system had.

As a pharmacist, Doc Clarke had seen what narcotics like cocaine and opiates could do to the human body. What it could turn people into. How it killed their souls and robbed them of every trace of their humanity.

But this was something different. Something worse.

For Doc Clarke was one of the few people in the city who knew that a new narcotic had been sweeping through the underworld of the city for the past month. A drug so powerful that it was turning normally docile, pathetic addicts into desperate lunatics, ready to do almost anything to get enough money for their next fix.

The police had done a fine job of keeping the problem out of the papers as they hunted the source of the new epidemic. But so far, the source had proven elusive.

Doc remembered the look in the robber's eyes when he spoke of Him. A kind of desperate reverence when he spoke of the man who had sold him this terrible drug.

A reverence that had made the hairs on the back of Doc's neck stand on end.

Doc flinched when the bell above the door to the pharmacy tinkled as the door opened. But he quickly relaxed when he saw Dave Small walk in, lugging a large parcel that obstructed his view. In all the excitement, Doc had forgotten he'd sent Dave to the post office to pick up a package from the post office a little over an hour before.

"I'm back," Dave called out with his usual cheerfulness as he heeled the door closed behind him. "I don't know what you ordered here, but whatever it is weighs a ton."

But Dave's mood quickly darkened when he saw Doc crouched beside the prone gunman on the floor. He set the parcel on the counter before he dropped it. "What happened?"

Doc nodded toward the door. "Flip the 'Open' sign to 'Closed' and pull down the shade," Doc told him. "I don't want anyone to see this."

Dave did what he'd been asked to do, then rushed to Doc's side. "What happened?"

"It was a hold up. A feeble attempt at one, but a hold up nonetheless."

"Jeez," Dave said as he pushed his hat further back on his head. "We've never had anyone try to stick us up before."

"This was more than just a simple stick up, Dave. Much more."

"Want me to call the police to come get him?"

But Doc had other plans. "Here, open the door to the lab while I carry him inside."

Doc picked up the junkie with an ease that surprised even him. The man was Doc's height—easily six feet tall – but weighed just over a hundred pounds. He was only skin and bones. And hunger. A damnable hunger that only a strange new powerful narcotic could feed.

Doc carried the husk of a man around the counter while Dave opened the door to the lab. While the door looked like a simple wood door to his customers, it was actually a steel hatch that concealed Doc Clarke's laboratory.

The lair of the Crimson Mask!

As Doc carried the man inside, the call light beneath the counter began to gently buzz once more.

"Uh oh," Dave said. "Looks like Commissioner Warrick is calling the Crimson Mask again."

"I know," Doc said as he carried the man inside. "And I'm already on the case."

Theodore Warrick, former commissioner of the New York Police Department, was not pleased by who he saw on his doorstep. A gaunt, disheveled young man with sunken, dark eyes. His skin had the sickly, yellowish tinge of the drug addicted.

"Hey, ya, mister," the young man said. "Can ya spare a couple of bucks for a guy down on his luck?"

Warrick drew himself up to his full height with an official bearing that was as impressive now as it had been back when he was in command of the largest police force in the nation. "I won't give you money, young man. But if it's food and warmth you're after, I'll see to it that you get both, so long as you conduct yourself accordingly."

Warrick stepped aside to permit this unfortunate young man access to his home.

After the young man slinked inside, he shook Warrick's hand in a most unique fashion. "Much obliged, mister. Much obliged."

Warrick made no effort to conceal his amazement, for there was only one other man in the world who could shake his hand in this secret way. The Crimson Mask!

"Good God, Bob!" Warrick cried. "I didn't even recognize you in that disguise."

"That's the general idea," Doc said, enjoying the look of surprise on his patron's face. "Thanks to you, I was taught by the best at L'Comédie Français."

Warrick had never doubted the money he'd spent on young Robert Clarke's education had been the best investment he'd ever made. Not only for Robert's sake, but for the sake of the city both men loved.

Bob Clarke's father had been Warrick's closest friend on the police force when he was brutally gunned down in the line of duty; shot in the head by gangsters during what the papers had called a routine patrol. But as Warrick—and every other cop in the city knew all too well—there was no such thing as a routine patrol. A policeman's death is always a harsh reminder of the dangers of their profession, their calling.

But out of the elder Clarke's tragic death sprang a new life; a life dedicated to fighting those who preyed upon the weak and vulnerable. A life dedicated willingly to putting an end to all those who sought to feed off the misery of others.

It was a fight that the young Robert Clarke had vowed to take up the moment he saw his father's lifeless body. His father had suffered the type of head wound that had caused the blood to pool around the eyes, giving the corpse something of a terrible crimson mask around the eyes.

That sight that had stayed with Bob Clarke every day since. It had stayed with him through his education and pharmacy school—which had been paid for by his father's benefits—and through his world travels paid for by his benefactor, Commissioner Warrick.

Upon his return to the city of his birth, Bob Clarke was no longer just a pharmacist or the son of a dead policeman. Instead, he was prepared to take up the mantle that had been left for him by his father. To use that lasting image of his dead father's body to strike fear into the hearts of the city's underworld. To become the Crimson Mask!

"I was growing concerned when you didn't answer my call," Warrick told him as they walked into his study. "You've never missed a call before."

"My pharmacy has never been held up before," Doc said, now walking and talking normally.

Warrick stopped short. "Held up? You? Why, I never thought that would happen. Sure, the neighborhood's not the best, but the people there adore you."

Doc sat in one of the plush chairs Warrick had in front of the fireplace. "This wasn't a local thug. He was a junkie who'd drifted downtown from some other part of the city. He was holding a gun on me when you called. Luckily, the buzzer and call light distracted him enough for me to get the gun safely away from him." Doc smiled. "Thanks for the help."

"My pleasure," Warrick said, absently. "Ironically enough, that's the very reason why I called you. This new narcotic that's been hitting the streets this past month has taken hold. This morning, a madman high on the stuff stormed into City Hall and it took four officers and all their strength to subdue him. Another one pulled a gun at the public library on Forty-Second Street and tried to hold up people in the main reading room. It only took three guards to subdue him."

Doc had feared this might happen a few weeks before when he'd first heard about the new drug. "And the police still haven't gotten any leads on where this drug is coming from?"

Warrick shook his head. "They've had every available man on the case and still haven't been able to come up with anything useful. The addicts we've been able to take into custody these past few weeks either die from withdrawal from the drug or are too incapacitated to tell us anything useful. This damnable poison they're using seems to scramble their senses to the point where they're reduced to a vegetative state. As you know, we've been successful in keeping all of this out of the press so far, but after what happened at City Hall and the library, it's becoming increasingly difficult to do so. Sooner or later, word will leak out and…"

"And as you're nowhere near finding out who the supplier is," Doc said, finishing the sentence for him, "it'll only put even more pressure on the police to work quickly, which will only make matters worse. It's a vicious circle."

Warrick continued. "The police lab has been trying to determine exactly what the narcotic is. Some of the best men in the nation have been working on it, but so far, they haven't had much luck."

"I know," Doc smiled. "But I have."

Slowly, Warrick smiled too. "You never cease to amaze me, Bob. How?"

"When you'd first told me about this crisis," Doc explained, "I knew it would only get worse before it got any better. I also knew that it would be a battle that would need to be fought in the laboratory as well as on the street. So I ordered some special equipment that might help me test the compound of the drug once I obtained a sample. In fact, Dave Small was at the post office picking up the equipment for me while I was being held up. Before I came here today, I was able to run a battery of tests on the junkie's blood to isolate the compound. That's why I wasn't able to answer your call right away."

"Well, don't keep me on tenterhooks, Doc," Warrick cried. "What did you find?"

"I ran two sets of tests and both came up conclusive," Doc said. "The drug in question is, at its base, heroin."

"Heroin?" Warrick repeated. "But we've had heroin addicts in this city for longer than I can remember. They've never acted out like this before."

"That's because they've never had this kind of heroin before," Doc said. "The needle marks on my hold-up man's arm show that this new drug is injected just like heroin, but it's more than that. It's a heroin-based narcotic that has been amplified to affect more parts of the brain than heroin normally does."

The look on Warrick's face told Doc he was losing the thread of what he was saying, so Doc put it another way. "I won't bore you with the scientific details, but think of it this way: Imagine that your brain is a Model T Ford with a small engine. Now remove the small engine and install an eight-cylinder engine in it. What do you think would happen to the Model T?"

Warrick thought for a moment. "I don't think it would fare too well for very long. It was never designed to handle that kind of power."

"Which is exactly the problem here," Doc explained. "The chemistry of this kind of heroin is very complex, but also very unstable. That's why it wreaks even more havoc on the systems of the people who take it."

"Which is why the people who take it die so quickly after becoming addicted," Warrick concluded as he lowered himself into the other chair at the fireplace. "Good God."

"It attacks the nerve centers of the brain that heroin usually attacks, only more so," Doc continued. "That's why users are beginning to do more reckless, unpredictable things. It also may be even more addictive, hence this rash of violent robbery attempts that have popped up all over the city in the past couple of days. It's only a theory," Doc admitted, "but I think it holds up given what we know."

Doc watched the gravity of the situation settle in Warrick's mind. He knew the former commissioner had seen more than his share of human depravity in his years on the force, but doubted he'd seen anything like this. Doc doubted anyone had.

Warrick shook himself out of it. "What do you suppose we do now? We haven't a moment to lose, but we still don't have any leads to go on!"

Doc pointed at his vagrant disguise. "That's where I come in. I'm going to pose as a drug addict to see if I can't infiltrate some of the drug dens. Maybe get a lead on where this poison is coming from. Sooner, rather than later, someone should be able to tell me something."

"I know you too well to doubt your methods," Warrick admitted, "but the department has had its best detectives on this case since the beginning and they haven't been able to find a single lead yet."

"They're good men," Doc smiled, baring a mouth full of false, decayed teeth. "But they're not the Crimson Mask."

Doc knew that Manhattan's Skid Row was just like the Skid Row of any major city in the world, only more so because, after all, this was New York.

Robert Clarke's classical education—for which Commissioner Theodore Warrick had generously paid—hadn't only been spent in classrooms and laboratories. For Doc's European studies had also taken him to the darkest back alleys of London and Manchester, the Rue Morgue of Paris and the post-Versailles cesspool that Berlin had slowly become. Doc studied these places because he'd known long ago that one did not learn how to fight crime by simply reading books or attending lectures on the subject. In order to tackle any disease—and crime was most certainly a disease—one had to study it up close and in its natural environment.

Robert Clarke had been an apt pupil.

He spent part of that afternoon skulking around the bars and flophouses

"It attacks the nerve centers of the brain …"

along the East River waterfront, easily blending in with the downtrodden crowd who frequented such places.

His disguise was flawless and he blended in with the legion of merchant seamen, drunkards and other reprobates who spent their meager means on cheap liquor and card games and other far more vile things. People paid Doc little notice and talked freely around the wretched little man. Doc managed to catch bits and pieces of various conversations while he sipped warm, stale beer. He didn't complain. He'd drunk far worse in his travels.

Of the many dens of iniquity Doc had visited that day, the place called the Ram's Head proved to be the most promising. After an hour or so of sitting at the bar, listening to a couple of drunken men talk about their dubious conquests and accomplishments, one topic caught Doc's interest: Magic Potion.

Both men spoke of it with a great reverence. The same kind of reverence that had made Doc's blood run cold when he'd heard the junkie speak of it earlier that day.

Doc paid closer attention as the two men discussed the matter further.

"I hear it makes you feel wonderful," said the bearded man next to Doc. "Makes you feel like you can do anything."

"I hear it's supposed to last for a long time, too," the other one said. "Make ya feel like ya don't have a care in the world."

Doc faked a drunken snicker and nudged the man on his right. "Now that's just the kinda stuff I'm lookin' for. They serve that stuff here?"

"Nah," the bearded man told him. "Drinkin' it don't do you much good. You gotta go to a special place for that kinda stuff. The kinda place that has needles and such on account of you havin' to inject it to feel anything. I stay out of them places on account of my bein' allergic to needles and such."

"Me too," said the other man, obviously feeling left out. "Never touch the stuff. Needles is bad business."

Doc gave them a sloppy smile as he rolled up his sleeve and showed them the fake needle marks he'd put on his arm. "You get used to 'em after a while. Say, I just got into town this mornin' and don't know nothin' from nowheres. Got any idea on where a fella like me might get some of that Magic Potion you two was talkin' about?"

It took Doc buying another round of beers to get the men to tell him what he wanted to know. The closest place for Magic Potion was an old warehouse just down the street off Pike's Slip near the tip of Manhattan. Doc knew whoever had chosen the location had chosen well. It was ideally situated to attract the downtrodden, yet far enough off the beaten path to minimize being accidentally discovered by the police.

Every instinct Doc had told him to notify Warrick of the location and have the police raid the place. But Doc also knew traditional methods hadn't gotten the police very far in finding out who was behind this dangerous brand of new narcotics.

It was time for the Crimson Mask to take over and try things his way.

Doc staggered toward the door of the warehouse and knocked. A faded lace curtain in a grimy window next to the door moved, but not enough for Doc to see who had moved it.

A moment later, the door flew open and a large, thick hand snatched Doc by the throat and pinned him against the wall. A bald, flat-faced man glared at him beneath thick eyebrows. "What do you want?"

Doc smiled, showing him his set of yellow, crooked teeth. "Whaddya think I want, friend? I wanna get well, see?" He showed him the false needle marks on his arm, knowing they were good enough to fool even an experienced drug peddler like this man.

The man looked at the arm, then let Doc go. "How did you find this place?"

"I asked around in a couple of places. They told me to come here."

The bald man took a step closer and glowered down at him. "Who?"

"You kiddin' me, friend?" Doc wiped nervously at his nose. "The kinda people who go to my kinda places don't exactly have callin' cards and they ain't big on givin' their names. Not the real ones, anyways." Then Doc threw in a twitch for good measure and said, "A couple of guys up at the Ram's Head told me this was a good place to find some Magic Potion. And I'm willin' to pay plenty for it, too."

The big man looked him up and down again. "How much?"

"I got enough." Doc smiled again. "Don't worry, sport. I'm a man of means."

The big man took him by the arm and shoved him inside. Doc tripped over a man passed out on the floor. He could've easily kept his balance, but let himself fall, knowing it would convince the big man he was really in a bad way.

The big man booted him in the pants and said, "Get up. There'll be plenty of time for layin' around soon enough."

Doc scrambled to his feet and started moving, stumbling through the maze of prone limbs and bodies of people who'd taken the Magic Potion. Doc figured there may have been as many as one hundred people or more in various stages of delirium scattered about the floor of the warehouse. Discarded human beings left on the floor to rot like sacks of flour.

Doc was glad the place was poorly lit. Otherwise the big man might've seen the look of pure disgust on his face.

The big man pushed him toward the front where an old man with long white hair and wire-rimmed spectacles sat at a flimsy wooden table beneath a weak yellow light.

"Got another customer for you, Hank," the big man said. "Says he wants some Potion."

"That so?" Hank said as he appraised Doc over his spectacles. "Yes, I imagine he does. He looks ripe enough, doesn't he?"

Judging from the man's accent, Doc doubted the man's name was actually Hank. Heinrick was probably much closer to the mark. It was the kind of accent Doc had heard before while studying psychology in Vienna. But why would a German be running a common drug den down on a Manhattan waterfront?

Doc pawed at his nose again and showed him his arm. "I'm ripe enough, boss. Don't you worry none."

The German looked at the phony needle marks and grinned a nasty grin. "Yes, I suppose you are." With a thin, pale hand, Hank opened a small drawer in the table and produced a small vial of clear fluid. He then took out a hypodermic needle and filled it with the liquid from the vial. "The first dose is free. The second is not. And, believe me, you'll want a second dose."

Doc widened his eyes greedily as the German placed the syringe on the desk. "That's…that's awfully generous of ya, boss."

The German's nasty grin got a bit nastier. "Not really. You'll buy a second dose and another and another. This is true Magic Potion we're selling here, friend. It'll carry you off to places you've never even dreamed existed. Places that you'll want to go back again and again, believe me." Then the German picked up the needle and handed it to Doc. "Your ticket to paradise. Enjoy the ride."

The German's grin disappeared at the sound of a loud knock at a door behind him somewhere in the darkness. Doc approximated where he was in relation to the warehouse and realized that door must lead out to the alley in the back.

Someone was paying a visit. And judging by the German's reaction, it was someone very important.

Doc wondered if this was the break he'd been waiting for. A connection to the source of this filthy poison.

The German closed the drawer as he got up from his desk and said to the big man: "Find him a spot somewhere on the floor. Keep an eye on things until my return."

Doc scooped up the syringe as the big man took him by the collar and steered him through the maze of wretched humanity toward one of the few vacant spots on the floor. He released Doc with a shove and Doc let himself fall once again, cradling his fragile parcel as if it were fine crystal.

Doc leaned back against the wall and placed the syringe on his lap. He was surprised that the big man was still there, looming over him.

"Thanks, friend," Doc said up to him. "I'm all set now."

But the bald man shook his large head. "Not yet, friend. We've got rules here, see, and the rules say we have to make sure you're not a cop. That's why I have to watch you shoot it. Right now."

Doc had no intention of putting that needle anywhere near his skin, much less injecting himself with that poison. He faked a twitch and said, "I kinda like to take my time, ya know? Ease into it a little in my own way."

The big man shrugged. "It's your trip. Take all the time you want." He crossed his massive arms in front of his chest. "I've got all night."

Stalling for time, Doc set the needle on his lap again and made a show of rolling up his left sleeve. In the darkness of the warehouse, he managed to steal a quick glance to where the German had been sitting. He noticed the back door and could tell that it was open.

Doc knew he and the big man were the only two sober people in the entire warehouse.

Doc flexed his left arm and flicked the vein where he'd placed the false needle marks. As the vein rose, Doc took the needle and heard the big man say, "That's it. Now just …"

Doc stabbed the needle into the meat of the big man's leg and injected the full vial into his system.

The big man stumbled back, clutching his leg as Doc leapt to his feet. He head-butted the man before he could cry out, shattering his nose with his forehead. Doc swept the big man's legs out from under him and eased him down slowly onto the floor, knowing a thud might alert the German to what was happening.

Doc climbed on top of the big man, pinning his thick shoulders to the floor while the drug took effect. From the analysis he'd done on the compound back at his lab, he knew it would be only a few moments before the powerful man was as incapacitated as the rest of the addicts in the warehouse.

When the big man's eyes fluttered before rolling up white into his head, Doc was glad—but not surprised—that his analysis had been correct.

Doc left the big man where he lay and crept toward the open doorway at the back of the warehouse. He pressed himself flat against the wall and got as close to the door as he dared. He closed his eyes and listened.

Hank and another man in the alley were speaking in German. They were probably speaking in their native tongue to prevent anyone from overhearing their conversation.

Unfortunately for them, the Crimson Mask happened to be fluent in German.

"When can I expect the next shipment?" the one called Hank asked.

"Tomorrow morning," the other man said. "Or the following day, at the latest."

"That is not good enough. As I've told you many times before, we must have more product! Demand is almost outpacing our supply. Tell him we'll need to increase our production significantly if he wants our plans to work."

"I've already spoken to Him," the second man explained, "but these things take time, Heinrick. You above all people should understand this by now."

"Nonsense!" Heinrick spat. "If you can't convince Him, then I will have to do it for you. Where is He? In Berlin?"

"No, He doesn't go back home until tomorrow night. But talking to Him won't do any good. As I've told you, this isn't a matter of …"

"Please do not attempt to lecture me on the business of narcotics, Albert. I have been in this business since before you were even born. The drug has been more effective than our wildest expectations and we must have more! Just tell Him I want to meet Him as soon as possible or everything we have accomplished may be for naught. When I call you in the morning, I will expect you to tell me where and when the meeting will take place. Now go. You have work to do and so do I."

Doc crept back into the shadows of the warehouse as he heard Heinrick walking back down the alley. Once the drug peddler had come back inside and locked the door behind him, Doc sprang on the old man from behind, covering his mouth so he couldn't cry out to the big man for help.

"Good evening, Heinrick," Doc said in German, mimicking Heinrick's own voice, hoping the ruse would disorient him. "Don't bother screaming because no one else can hear you. Your big friend is on his way to dreamland, so it's only you and me now."

Doc released his hand just enough to let the man speak. "Who…who are you?"

Doc placed his hand back over the old man's mouth as he pulled him back toward the desk. "Who I am isn't important. But who you are and what you're doing is very important to me." Then he took an empty syringe from the desk drawer and held it to the old man's neck. "And you're going to tell me."

"I…I am no one," Heinrick sputtered. "No one at all. Just a simple cog in a very large wheel doing my part."

"Don't sell yourself so short," Doc told him. "You sounded pretty important when you were talking to your friend just now. Albert is his name, isn't it?" He let Heinrick see the empty syringe. He let him see him thumb back the empty plunger. "Who was he?"

"Albert," Heinrick sputtered. "Albert Mueller. He is my link to the supplier of the drug."

"And who is the supplier?" Doc scrapped the tip of the needle against the exposed skin of Heinrick's neck. "And don't tell me you don't know because that would make me very angry."

"I…I only know Albert, I swear it!" Heinrick said. "I swear on my life. The supplier is a mystery to everyone, maybe even Albert. I've met him a few times, yes, but always at a time and place of his choosing. You were listening at the door, then you know I can't get in touch with him directly."

"Perhaps," Doc allowed, "but you certainly know how to get in touch with Albert, don't you?"

"Of…of course. His information is in the notebook. In the drawer. I can find it for you if you …"

Doc jerked the German's head back at a harsher angle, exposing his neck even further as he placed the syringe on the desk and fumbled inside the drawer for the notebook. He found it and held it up for Heinrick to see. "What is his number listed under?" He put more pressure on Heinrick's throat. "And if you lie, I'll know it. Then I'll pump that empty needle right into your coroided artery. And I think a man like you knows what happens to someone when an air bubble hits an artery, don't you Heinrick?"

"...that would make me very angry."

"I will not lie," Heinrick said, then proceeded to tell him the name and number where Alfred could be reached.

With his free hand, Doc thumbed through the notebook and found the entry, exactly where he said it would be.

"You see?" Heinrick gave a desperate smile. "I told you the truth. About Albert. About the supplier. You let me go now?"

But Doc's grip held. "Not before you tell me about these plans. These expectations you mentioned."

"Our expectations?" Heinrick repeated. He surprised Doc by actually laughing. "Our expectations are to exploit your American weaknesses, my friend. Our expectations are that you are all weak and your weakness is a hunger to escape reality. To destroy yourselves. We aren't simply feeding that hunger. We're expanding it." Heinrick stopped laughing. "Our expectations are that you will die and there is nothing you can do to stop us!"

Doc picked up the empty syringe and plunged the needle into the dope peddler's neck, depressing the plunger and sending an air bubble straight into his system. "I just did."

Doc shoved the German against the wall and left the dope peddler to die in agony on the floor.

"It's a good thing you called us when you did," Warrick told Doc when they were back in Warrick's study later that evening. "The police were able to rescue ninety-seven unfortunates in that warehouse last night. They're all receiving the best of care even as we speak."

"Ninety-seven?" Doc asked. "I counted more than that."

"I know you did," Warrick said. "The rest were either already dead or beyond saving." He offered Doc a grim smile. "That's the problem with this line of work, Bob. There are damned few happy endings. Damned few indeed."

Doc knew it all too well. "Do the police think anyone saw them remove the addicts from the warehouse?"

"Thanks to your instructions, no," Warrick said. "They didn't think anyone was watching the warehouse anyway, but proceeded with an abundance of caution by having detectives remove the unfortunates in livery trucks, not police trucks or ambulances. That should've eased the suspicion of anyone in the neighborhood."

"That's good." Doc was glad the ninety-seven addicts were now receiving the treatment they needed, but the deaths of the other unfortunates troubled him deeply. Heinrick's death had been justified, but even his death hardly balanced the scales of justice.

The Crimson Mask knew he still had plenty of work to do before the night was out.

Doc asked Warrick: "Were you able to get an address on that phone number I'd given you from Heinrick's notebook?"

"I was." Warrick checked a notepad on his desk. "The telephone company said the exchange belongs to a John Smith in the Parker Building over on Columbus Avenue. Penthouse apartment."

"John Smith, eh?" Doc said. "How original."

"You didn't expect the man to have the place under his real name, did you? Do you want me to have him arrested?"

"No," Doc said. "I think it's time for the Crimson Mask to pay him a visit instead."

After a quick visit to his lab to change into regular clothes and pick up a few essential items, the Crimson Mask took to the streets at around midnight.

He was careful to make sure the brim of his fedora cast his face in shadow as he took a cab to the Parker Building up on Columbus Avenue. He doubted the driver would ever be asked to identify him, but Doc always preferred to be safer rather than sorry in the long run.

The Parker Building had been one of the most impressive apartment buildings in the city when it had been built twenty years before. Now that a neighborhood had grown up around it, it looked just like any other such building in town.

Once he paid his fare, Doc waited until the cab had turned the corner before trying to find a way upstairs. A doorman and a porter were lazing about the lobby, chatting while they read the late edition of that day's newspaper. And although Doc had no doubt he could subdue both of them, he knew they would be discovered by one of the tenants returning home from a night on the town.

Luckily for him, the Crimson Mask was accustomed to finding ways into buildings other than the front door.

He crept around to the back of the building and found a set of fire escape stairs. But the ladder was locked and secured about ten feet above the ground, far too high for a normal man to reach.

But as many had learned before, the Crimson Mask was not a normal man.

Years of studying ancient stretching techniques from the Near and Far

East had made Doc more agile and stronger than even most professional athletes. He found a small, but firm handhold in the masonry of the building and then another, climbing just high enough to lunge for the locked ladder.

Doc made it with ease and began his quiet ascent toward the penthouse apartment where Albert Mueller lived. He moved quickly, but lightly; careful not to make any noise that might awaken any of the sleeping residents as he went.

When he got to the top of the fire escape, he realized, much to his surprise, that the stairs did not go all the way up to the roof. They stopped one whole floor below!

Doc flexed his fingers once more before digging them into the masonry and slowly pulling himself up, using only his trained fingers to do so. Slowly, but steadily, he reached the top. He pulled himself up just over the ledge to see if anyone was on the roof.

He spotted a broad, thick man with close-cropped grey hair sitting in a chair off to his far left, smoking a cigar and enjoying the view of the jagged Manhattan skyline. Like a man who didn't have a care in the world.

Like a man who didn't know his life was about to change.

Doc sensed this man was far too relaxed to be a guard. He knew this man must live there, and must be the same man who met Heinrick in the alley only a few hours before: Albert Mueller.

Doc was glad that the entire rooftop was dark, save for the ambient light of the Manhattan skyline. He silently pulled himself over the ledge and dropped to a crouch on the other side. He listened for other voices nearby. For footsteps on the rooftop gravel.

Hearing nothing, he produced a syringe from an inside pocket of his suit jacket and crept toward the man.

When he got close enough, Doc slipped his left hand over Albert's forehead as he drove the needle into the back of his neck with his right and injected the contents of the syringe into Albert's system.

The man tried to get to his feet, but Doc pushed him back down in the chair until he and the chair pitched backward down to the rooftop gravel.

With one hand, Doc easily pinned him prone on the ground as he slipped on his newest invention—a phosphorescent mask that glowed a deep crimson in the dark!

The shock of the silent assault—which had happened in a matter of seconds—had disoriented the German to the point where he was beyond crying out. And the terrible glowing crimson mask bearing down on him from the darkness of the night sky only added to his terror.

"Good evening, Herr Mueller," the Crimson Mask said in German. "You do not know who I am, but I know who you are. You are the man responsible for peddling the poison that is destroying this city. My city. The same poison I injected into your system just now."

Albert's eyes widened in wild terror.

The Crimson Mask smiled. "Well, it's not exactly the same kind of poison. I managed to make some changes to the solution. Some very painful changes. Now, I happen to have a serum which will countermand the drug, but I'll only give it to you if you do exactly what I say."

Albert whimpered as he began to squirm, but the Mask held him firm. "I know you were with Heinrick tonight at the warehouse. But Heinrick's dead and you will be too unless you tell me who your supplier is."

"I…I can't," Albert responded in German. "I can't do that. He'll kill me if I do!"

The Crimson Mask spoke directly into his ear. "And I'll let you die if you don't; only it'll be a far, far more painful death than anything he'll do to you."

"I…I don't know how to reach him," Albert stammered.

"You're lying!" yelled the Crimson Mask. "I heard what you said in the alley. You were going to arrange a meeting with Heinrick, so I know you can get in touch with the supplier if you want to. And in a few short minutes, you'll be in so much pain, you'll be begging to tell me. But by then, I won't be able to help you."

Albert's breathing became shallow, erratic. "I…I don't have a name, only a number that I use to call him. I …"

The Crimson Mask put more weight on Albert's chest. "You don't have this kind of time to waste. Feel that twinge in your stomach right now? That's the toxin beginning to take effect. The pain will start any moment now."

The German's eyes watered and his lips trembled as the impending torture grew closer. He couldn't get the words out fast enough. "I…I… really don't know his true name. You have to believe me!"

"Perhaps," the Crimson Mask allowed, "but you really do know where he is, don't you?"

"He…he is living in a mansion…in Westchester," Albert sputtered, "but it's too well guarded. You'll never …"

Albert shrieked as the terrible glowing crimson mask shot even closer to his face. "Let me worry about that. What's the address?"

Theodore Warrick drove along the narrow country roads toward The Supplier's Westchester mansion while the Crimson Mask loaded his revolver in the back seat.

By then, he'd also changed his phosphorescent crimson mask for his traditional crimson silk one.

"You know I never question your methods," Warrick said over his shoulder to Doc. "But I still don't know how you got Mueller to tell you where the supplier was."

"By the oldest and most effective methods around," Doc admitted with more than a hint of pride. "Terror mixed with a dash of suggestion. I told him I'd just injected him with a higher potency of his own heroin, designed to cause him great pain. Then I convinced him the fear he was experiencing was the drug going to work on his system."

Warrick was confused. "But how did you have time to do that between the time you left my house and saw Albert?"

"I didn't," Doc smiled. "I took some sodium pentothal from my lab and injected him with that instead. I imagine that he'll actually feel pretty good when he wakes up in a few hours."

"Amazing." Warrick shook his head in amazement as he steered through the narrow, tree-lined road. "But I must ask you why you killed Heinrick, but left Albert alive?"

"If Heinrick had enough influence to meet with The Supplier directly, he was too important to this operation to be allowed to live," Doc explained. "But Albert is nothing more than a high paid messenger boy. And after I take down The Supplier tonight, Albert will deliver another kind of message to all the others involved in this conspiracy: to keep their poison out of New York."

"Indeed," Warrick said. "Did he happen to tell you how many men are guarding The Supplier's house?"

Doc finished loading his revolver, then snapped the cylinder closed. "No, but I'll find out soon enough."

Warrick stood guard in the car from the road while Doc approached The Supplier's mansion on foot through the woods. The moon shone high and full through the barren branches of the forest, giving him good light to go by. The wind had picked up as well, concealing the sound of snapping twigs or rustling leaves as he made his way toward the house.

Doc stopped when he came upon a stone wall and spotted the grand mansion bathed in moonlight in the clearing beyond. That same moonlight—which had been his ally in the woods—had suddenly become his enemy in the clearing as he could easily be spotted if he approached the mansion. There wasn't so much as a shrub or a bush in the acre or so between the stone wall and the house to provide him cover.

That had probably been one of the reasons why The Supplier had chosen this house in the first place.

Doc crouched behind the stone wall and observed the situation. Other than a light from a room on a window on the third story, the house was in complete darkness. That didn't deter him, for even if The Supplier wasn't home, there might be vital information about the heroin operation to be gathered in that house.

The Crimson Mask was going in, one way or the other.

He checked the roof for sentries that might be posted there, but saw no sign of any. Next he looked down the long roadway leading toward the main gate for signs of guards. Other than one man in the small guardhouse, he didn't see anything there either.

He was about to hop the wall and make a run for the mansion when he spotted a guard coming around from the back of the house, flashlight in hand sweeping the darkness. Doc knew he was out of the beam's range, so he wasn't worried about being detected.

But he knew he'd have to deal with this man first before attempting to enter the mansion.

Doc stayed low against the wall as he moved to his left as the guard continued walking toward his right. Once they'd passed each other, Doc leapt the wall and ran toward the guard at an angle as quickly and as quietly as he could from behind.

The benefits of such open ground was that there were no trees or twigs to sound his approach. And he hoped the wind would muffle his footfalls as he ran.

Doc slowed to a jog as he caught up with the guard from behind. He delivered a knife-edged chop to the side of the man's neck just as he sensed someone was behind him. The guard dropped to the ground out cold.

Doc switched off the guard's flashlight and dragged the unconscious man against the wall of the house. It wasn't the most ideal hiding place, but it was the best he could do given the circumstances.

Doc was about to look for more guards when he was tackled hard from behind. The blow left him dazed for a moment until he felt a searing pain

"He delivered a knife-edged chop …"

deep in the shin of his left leg. He cleared his head and found a German Shepherd had taken hold of his leg.

He'd encountered these killers before; dogs trained by their owners to attack intruders in silence—without barking or growling—for one purpose only: to kill.

Doc kicked out at the dog with his free leg, connecting with the animal's snout. When the dog released his bite, Doc knew the animal was trained to lunge for his throat next.

The dog recovered quickly and did just that, rearing back on its haunches before launching itself for the kill, baring its sharp canine teeth.

Doc had braced for the attack and brought up his forearm beneath the lunging dog's jaw, thwarting the attack. The animal snarled and drooled as he tried to lunge down to get at Doc's throat. Doc held the animal at bay as he felt for the guard's flashlight on the ground. When he found it, he slammed it against the side of the animal's skull.

The German Shepherd dropped to the ground, as unconscious as the guard.

Doc knew all too well how dangerous dog bites could be. The germs that were commonplace in any dog's mouth could be deadly to humans if left untreated for a long period of time. Unfortunately, he didn't have time to worry about such things. He simply took off his tie and made the best tourniquet he could manage in the time he had. He made a mental note to check for any first aid supplies in the house.

Doc scrambled to his feet and, somewhat hobbled, worked his way to the back of the house from where the guard had come. All of the windows he passed were too high for him to attempt entry without breaking the glass. And despite his run-in with the guard and the dog, Doc had every reason to believe he still had the element of surprise on his side.

He crept around to the back of the house and found the ground rose higher there, making it easier to reach the windows. He sneaked a quick look inside, but all he saw was a large, dark room.

A good point of entry.

Doc tried the window, but of course, it was locked from the inside. He opened the hidden pocket in his suit and produced a small leather case that contained, among other things, a thin strip of solid steel. He slipped the strip in between the two windows and slid the locks open.

Slowly, quietly, he eased up the window until he had just enough space to slide inside. Doc was about to close the window again to avoid detection by any other guards who might be roaming the premises.

And that's when he heard the unmistakable click of a hammer being thumbed back on a pistol.

A voice called out to Doc from the darkness. "Don't move."

The words were in English, but held a heavy German accent. Doc responded in German. "Is that any way to treat a guest?"

A light came on and Doc found himself standing in an oversized, wood-paneled den cluttered with overstuffed furniture and other expensive furnishings.

Doc saw a thick, heavy-set man in a silk smoking jacket sitting behind an even larger oak antique desk. And he was aiming a .38 right at Doc's stomach.

"A masked intruder breaking into my home in the wee hours of the morning," the man said in English. He laughed, but his gun remained aimed at Doc's belly. "How wonderfully dramatic. Like something from an opera."

"Like something from Wagner, perhaps?" Doc responded in German, hoping to confuse the man with the gun.

The German shook his head. "Too subtle for Wagner," the man said in English. "I must compliment you on your accent, Herr Intruder. It's almost perfect, but your tones stick at the back of your throat, even if only a little. A native German would give them full pronunciation from within; from the soul as is our right and privilege." He breathed in deep, as if to demonstrate his lung capacity. "Still, you've learned to imitate my language well," then added, "for an American, anyway."

Doc stepped further into the room, careful to keep his hands loose at his sides and in plain view. He knew his own gun might've been too high on his hip to be drawn, but it was also out of the German's sight. "I take it you're The Supplier everyone has been telling me about."

"The Supplier?" The thick German surprised Doc by laughing. Cackling was closer to it, really. "Is that really what they call me?" He shook his head. "Say what you will about Germans, my friend, but we are quite a literal people." Then his laugh went back to wherever it came from. "How did you mange to find me?"

Doc refused to give him the satisfaction of an answer. He only hoped Warrick was close enough to hear the shot if The Supplier pulled the trigger. "It wasn't difficult. Your organization isn't nearly as advanced as you'd like to believe it to be."

"Organization?" the German repeated. "Is that your word or their's?"

"Mine," Doc said. "That's what it is, isn't it?"

"Do you really think this is simply just another petty drug ring?" The Supplier asked. "Another mindless criminal enterprise seeking to make money and nothing more?" He shook his head. "Why, if that's all we were, your police would've thrown us in irons by now, wouldn't they?" The German sucked his teeth. "Such linear thinking. How very American. You haven't the slightest idea of our true purpose, do you?"

It was Doc's turn to smile. "People like you often say it's about more than money, but that's what it comes down to in the end. Always."

"I'm sorry to disappoint you, but in this instance, our success and wealth will be measured by a different form of currency than that to which you are accustomed."

"Reichsmarks, I'd wager," Doc stated.

Once again, the German shook his head. "A currency that can't be kept in a vault or traded in the open market, but that can buy what we seek for the price of inexpensive chemicals. That currency is Anarchy. Chaos. It's a currency your country has never really known, but will know all too well and soon enough. The seed has already taken root and will only grow more and more until we have achieved what we want: to help your people to destroy yourselves from within. And we'll use the weakest amongst you to do it."

It was quite a bit for Doc to take in, especially with a gun aimed at his belly. "That will never happen."

The German smiled again. "It already has. And there's very little that you or anyone else can do to stop it. The numbers of addicts grow more and more in number by each passing day. Soon, no one will be able to stop us, but for now …"

Doc saw the glint in the German's eye and heard the tone in his voice just before he squeezed the trigger. Just in time for Doc to dive behind a couch to his right as the glass in the window behind where he'd been standing shattered.

"Come, come, my friend," the German called out to him. "There's no need to make this even more painful than it has to be. You're cornered with nowhere to go. You …"

With surprising agility, the Crimson Mask sprang up from behind the couch and fired three times in rapid succession. Each of the three bullets found a home deep in the center of the German's chest.

The Supplier dropped the gun as he fell back into his chair, sending it rolling back behind the desk and against the wall.

Doc leapt over the couch and rushed to the man's side, listening for footsteps of guards or anyone running toward the sound of the shot.

The German was dying by the time Doc reached him. But not even impending death could wipe that damnable smile from his face. "You… needn't worry, my friend. There's no one else here. There's no need." He coughed a wet cough that Doc knew must be due to the blood filling his lungs. "I'm not important enough…to warrant more than two guards."

Doc saw The Supplier was beginning to fade and he jerked him awake. "Who are you? Who do you work for?"

The German's smile faded as his jaw went slack. "It…doesn't… matter…I…don't matter. You've ended only my…life today. Nothing… more. I only wish I could've lived…to see the glory of …"

And with that, The Supplier died.

The Crimson Mask was busy tending to his wounded leg while Theodore Warrick examined the contents of The Supplier's desk.

"Astounding," the former police commissioner said. "Absolutely astounding. Shipping records, ledgers, even maps of every major city in the United States. All of it is in German, of course, but I have a feeling we'll be able to cut through that soon enough. The FBI will have to be alerted too, of course, but we'll finish them off." Warrick looked at his protégé with no small measure of pride. "You've not only done your city a great service, Bob, but your country as well."

"I hope so," Doc Clarke said as he placed gauze on his wound, then began to wrap the bandage around his leg.

"Say, what's the matter with you?" Warrick asked. "You've just helped unravel a major drug syndicate here tonight. Why, with the information we have here, we'll be able to put a stop to these criminals but fast."

"I'm not so sure," Doc said. "The Supplier said he didn't care much about money and I have to say I believe him. He spoke of spreading anarchy and chaos and how it all served some kind of greater purpose. He died before I could find out what that purpose was. But even if he'd lived, I doubt he would've said more."

Warrick rapped his knuckles against one of the ledgers on the desk. "He'll be telling us plenty in what we've found here tonight. That's one of those lessons about crime fighting that you need to remember, Bob. We don't always have the luxury of worrying about tomorrow. Sometimes we can only worry about today."

The Crimson Mask usually agreed with his patron.

But on that evening, with the sound of the German's warning still fresh in his ears, he wasn't so sure.

The End

It's All Fortier's Fault

The reason why I wrote this story is because Ron Fortier suggested it.

Although I've been a fan of classic pulp fiction for a while, I'd never heard of the Crimson Mask before Ron mentioned he was looking to put together an anthology based on the character. Ron encouraged me to continue writing short stories in between my standard novel-length manuscripts, so I decided to look at the guidelines he'd sent me on the character.

Out of all the anthologies Airship 27 was looking to publish, the Crimson Mask appealed to me most because he seemed to have all of the elements of the iconic pulp characters without such a defined presence in the reader's consciousness.

Because the three novels I currently have on the market—PROHIBITION, FIGHT CARD: AGAINST THE ROPES and SLOW BURN—are all set in 1930s New York City, I was already comfortable with the time period. I had done plenty of research on that part of our country's history, but this story gave me a certain freedom I didn't have in my usual writing. I didn't have to rely on historic accuracy and, instead, could create my own story within the generous parameters of the existing Crimson Mask character.

I bought the Crimson Mask anthology that Altus Press published a couple of years ago, so I could get a sense of how the character worked. I was also looking for something that hadn't been done in other stories so I could contribute something unique to the Crimson Mask canon.

The result is the story you've read and hopefully enjoyed. I know I had a lot of fun doing it.

TERRENCE P. McCAULEY won TruTV's *Search for the Next Great Crime Writer* Contest in 2008. His Quinn novella, "Against the Ropes" will be published as part of the successful FIGHT CARD series in early 2013. Three Quinn short stories are currently available in the following anthologies: "A Brave New World," as part of ATOMIC NOIR, published by Out Of the Gutter Online as part of Noircon 2012; "Lady Madeline's Dive," as part of THUGLIT; and "Blood Moon of 1931" in Matt Hilton's ACTION: PULSE POUNDING TALES. All works are available on Amazon.com. McCauley's 1932 murder mystery, "The Slow Burn," will be published by Noir Nation Books in 2013. A proud native of the Bronx, NY, he is currently working on his next novel. He can be found on Twitter: @tmccauley_nyc; on Facebook at https://www.facebook.com/TerrencePMcCauley; and at terrencepmccauley@gmail.com by email.

THE MYSTERY MAN
by Gary Lovisi

The man in the bed tossed and turned in heated delirium, unable to sleep, his mind lost in a miasma of dark fearful nightmare. That man was Robert Clarke, Ph.G., pharmacist, also known as Doc Clarke by the local people of the poor East Side neighborhood where he had his drug store—but he also had a secret identity. Bob Clarke was the city's ace crime fighter, the nemesis of violent gangsterism known as the Crimson Mask.

Clarke's nightmare vision was one that he relived often in his dreams. It was a replay of what had occurred years before. His father had been a dedicated and decorated New York City policeman. One of New York's finest. A police sergeant who had been killed in the line of duty by rampaging gangsters. Young Bob had seen his father die, gunned down from behind like a dog, and he had seen the bullets fired into the back of his father's head by an unknown assailant as he lay on the ground defenseless. It was a terrible image for the then young college student to witness. Even more terrible and bizarre was the fearsome appearance of his dying father's face to the lad, for the slugs that entered the police sergeant's brain had caused a strange and unique occurrence. There was, for one spilt second, an unaccountable rush of blood into his father's face —and that face formed a perfect and stark mask of bright red blood. A crimson mask. The image manifested itself into the son's very soul and had affected him deeply. Young Bob Clarke never forgot what he had seen in his father's dying face that terrible night. No one was ever arrested for his father's murder. That image had been burned into young Clarke's brain forever after.

Bob Clarke screamed in rage and awoke from his nightmare with grim determination. His heart racing, his fear and anger stoked by reliving that terrible event of years before—but mostly all that remained was an aching sadness for the loss of his slain father—a man whom he had loved and respected. Clarke missed his father and on that night long ago he had vowed to use all the power at his command to fight crime and to bring down violent gangsterism. Thus, the Crimson Mask was born.

Clarke wiped the sweat from his face. He hadn't had that dream about his father in many weeks and knew that it must presage some dire forthcoming major crime event. It was almost as if Clarke had some uncanny second sight when it came to crime, that he could sense the trouble brewing even before it had fully developed, but this awareness was much more down-to-earth than mere feelings. Clarke was a man who forever had his ear to the murmurings of the criminal class, to local rumor, to the talk out on the street in his poor neighborhood, and to his keen knowledge of events that were happening and reported in the news every day. Bob Clarke was the type of man who had a sharp intuition, he could see what was behind the headlines, understand what was written behind the sentences that made up newspaper stories and police reports. Sometimes what was not said or written there could be more interesting and more important than what was.

Clarke sighed deeply. It was already another sunny morning in the city he loved. Time to get up out of bed and get dressed, maybe meet Dave or Sandy for a quick breakfast and then get down to work at his drug store on the East Side. That was what was on the surface of things in his life most days, his normal, seemingly daily routine at his drug store or the hospital, a day like most others, but behind the scenes Bob could smell the bile and pus of criminal planning and wicked schemes that would soon be set in motion. He knew the Crimson Mask would need to be called into action again very soon.

The man waited patiently for the bank to open for the day's business. He was already in disguise. He carefully examined his expensive woolen suit jacket, made sure his tie was knotted carefully and positioned properly, and then hefted the briefcase held in his left hand. It was not very heavy. He smiled victoriously and checked his watch, it was now 8:59 a.m. One more minute and the bank would open. Then his name would go down in criminal history. He briefly wondered what name the newspapers would give him in their stories—he certainly hoped it would be something suitably creative and evocative, in keeping with his amazing crime.

David Small, wearing his white pharmacist jacket, smiled with a glow that showed his healthy pink cheeks to the elderly customer who had come into the drug store to have a prescription filled. Dave knew the man was a local fellow, retired many years and a veteran of the Great War that ended in 1918, but none of that mattered to him, nor to his boss, Doc Clarke. For when it came to helping the local people of this poor neighborhood they served, they saw each person as one of their own, and all were valued friends and neighbors.

"There's a new price on these pills, Mr. James," Dave told his customer suddenly.

The old man frowned with dismay, "I don't think I can afford it, son." He knew what that 'new price' talk meant. He looked down at the small amount of money in his hand wondering if it would be enough. He knew that it would not be. He was poor and medicine cost a lot these days, but he needed the pills desperately for his wife's heart condition. "Everything seems to be going up in price these days, young man. Why am I not surprised?"

David Small could not resist a friendly smile, "Well, not this time, Mr. James. It appears that today is your lucky day, because the new cost for your wife's medicine has actually gone down in price."

"Down? How can that be?" James replied astonished.

"Happens all the time, the market fluctuates, prices change, supply and demand they call it, sir," Dave said explaining the reason with a sly grin, totting up the order and presenting the old man with a bill for his wife's pills that was half of what it usually was. Half of what it should have been.

"My God! That's so much less than what I was paying for Alice's medicine! Are you sure your figures are correct, young man?"

Dave laughed gently, "Absolutely, sir. I'm very good at math. The new price will be in effect indefinitely," Dave added with a warm smile, for it did his heart good to help these old folks in their time of need.

"Well, well! Why, thank you so much young man," the old fellow said as he paid Dave Small and left the drug store with a big smile on his face. "Alice will be so happy to hear this. We'll be eating good tonight for once, too, because of it."

Dave watched the old veteran leave the store.

"I'll bet you he's going to take his Alice out to dinner tonight with the money you saved him," a voice spoke softly from behind David Small. "Married all these years and you can see they still love each other as much as when they were first hitched."

It was Doc Clarke, the owner of the pharmacy and a man whose heart was even bigger than Dave's own when it came to the poor of this local community.

"You caught me fair and square, Bob," Dave told his friend and boss quickly. "I was going to make up the difference from out of my own pay. I just can't charge that old man and his wife that price increase for the medicine she needs for her heart condition—so I gave him a price decrease. I know that drug is expensive, but they can not afford it."

Doc Clarke smiled indulgently, put a reassuring hand upon his assistant's shoulder, "No problem, Dave. Actually, I'm rather proud of you. That's just why I opened this drug store here, to serve the community and to help the poor. Mr. James and his wife, Alice, are two of the best and most needy. They deserve our help."

Dave offered a slight nod. "It kinda makes me feel good, you know, Bob?"

"I know, Dave, me too," Clarke admitted to his friend. Dave worked at Doc Clarke's pharmacy when needed. Dave Small was the son of a wealthy family, but was devoted to his friend and helped him in his various activities whenever he could.

Now that Mr. James had gone and the store was empty the two men were alone. Dave got down to what was his real interest. "So what's next on the agenda, Boss?"

Dave Small was one of what Clarke called his loyal triumvirate—one of only three people in the world who knew the secret identity of the Crimson Mask—and that in fact, the ace crime fighter was the pharmacist, Robert Clarke, also known as Doc Clarke by the locals. The other two people were Theodore Warrick, former police commissioner, and Sandra Gray, a young beauty who worked as a nurse's aide at City Hospital. Ted and Dave were old friends devoted to Bob Clarke. Sandy could handle a gun and was a skilled driver, but she was also deeply in love with Clarke. Bob loved her deeply as well, but he was too obsessed with continuing his war on crime in the memory of his murdered father. Because of her love for him, Sandy was willing to wait for the day when the Crimson Mask retired so that she and Bob could be together as husband and wife. In the meantime, Bob waged his one-man war on crime, and Sandy and the others helped in any way they could.

"Well, Boss, what's up?" Dave Small repeated his question.

"Nothing concrete I fear, Dave. I haven't received a call from Warrick yet, no red signal either," Clarke replied with a hint of disappointment. Clarke had installed a special red light in his store that was connected to Theodore Warrick's home. When this light flashed red, that was the signal that the Crimson Mask was needed and for him to get in touch with the former police commissioner. At other times, Warrick would just phone Clarke at the store on a special secure phone line, but as yet there had been no contact. Clarke was disappointed that there seemed to be no pressing need for the services of the Crimson Mask, but he knew the wheels of crime were turning and churning even at that very moment and that something was always in the works.

"I hope we'll see some action soon, Boss," Dave said enthusiastically, champing at the bit to get to see action on what he considered his real job—doing crime fighting work for the Crimson Mask.

"No one is more anxious to get the Crimson Mask into action than I am," Clarke stated grimly, as he picked up a newspaper and pointed out an article to his assistant. "Here's something interesting. Read this and tell me what you think of it."

Dave Small picked up the paper that was open to a full page article about a daring bank robbery the day before that was said to be a great mystery to the police.

"'Police Baffled By Bank Heist,'" Dave Small read the headline out loud, "It looks like just the thing for the Crimson Mask."

"I was thinking the same thing, Dave, but read the entire article."

Dave Small held up the paper and read the long article carefully. It was a detailed piece about a robbery at a Security National Bank branch on 42nd Street yesterday morning that had the police baffled. Somehow the bank vault had been breached but there was no sign of damage, only the safety deposit boxes had been touched. They had been most professionally rifled. A fortune in cash and jewelry stolen. No one had seen a thing. There was no sign of forced entry into the vault, nor the bank. No sign initially that the boxes had been rifled. It was a complete and utter mystery and the papers had already dubbed the master thief 'The Mystery Man.'

"This Mystery Man seems to have gotten away with a million dollars in cash and jewelry," Dave offered.

"Yes, that much or more. So what do you think?" Clarke asked.

"Sure seems strange to me, Boss. They say there is no sign of forced entry into the vault, or the bank. That's impossible. How can that be?"

"That's just what the Crimson Mask will find out."

Dave Small smiled, for now he knew that the Crimson Mask was going to get down to business!

After the Security National Bank branch on Lexington Avenue opened for business the next morning, a dapper young man carrying a briefcase calmly walked towards the front door of the bank. He was once again in disguise, and he walked past the armed bank guard, passed rows of tellers, passed the manager who gave him a slight nod of friendly customer greeting, and then right out the front door. He was soon lost among the myriad bodies walking down the busy Manhattan thoroughfare. He smiled as he left the bank, and at the name the newspapers had recently given him, calling him, 'The Mystery Man.' He liked that name. It was mysterious, just as he was.

Hours later, Security National Bank Branch Manager Miles Stanhope sat at his desk doing the weekly reports when he heard the loud screams coming from the back of the building. They came from over by the vault area. It was a woman, yelling wildly, shouting in anger, and he bolted to the scene of the disturbance to find his erstwhile assistant Harvey Kurtz desperately trying to console an agitated elderly female customer. Stanhope swallowed nervously at the impending problem, for he realized that the agitated woman was not just any bank customer, but she was none other than Mrs. Samuel Van Camp, wife of the wealthy industrialist and Democratic Party candidate for senator. Stanhope rushed over to his assistant and the bawling woman.

"Mr. Kurtz, what is the meaning of this?" Stanhope asked his assistant, not wanting to confront the woman directly yet because of her frantic condition.

"Oh, Mr. Stanhope, I am so glad to see you. Mrs. Van Camp's jewels have been stolen. Her safety deposit box has been opened and all her jewelry is gone!"

"That cannot be!" Stanhope blurted, but one look at the box door assured him it was. "Impossible!"

"My rare tiara with the Burma Emerald is gone, so are my diamond rings and necklaces, all gifts from my husband," Mrs. Van Camp cried loudly, a bit too loudly to be sure, and Stanhope and Kurtz were becoming quite nervous. The two men had no idea just how nervous they were going to get once they found out the truth of what had actually happened.

"They are priceless!" Mrs. Van Camp screamed. "Priceless! What kind of security do you have in this bank! Where have my jewels gone to!"

Branch Manager Stanhope and his assistant Mr. Kurtz tried to soothe the distraught woman but it was useless, so they immediately called the police and then her husband. News of the matter would, of course, make the newspapers, and in fact it was immediately broadcast on the midday news on the radio. It was a shocking robbery at a supposedly secure financial institution, which shook the wealthy to their core.

It was over the radio where Bob Clarke heard the news of that second robbery. It was while he was on his way to the Security National branch on 42nd Street, the bank that had been robbed the day before. Clarke had immediately left his drug store to investigate the first robbery, keeping Dave back at the store so it would be open and operating. It did not look good if every time Clarke ran to a crime scene—or when the Crimson Mask was in action—that the drug store was closed. It might cause undue suspicion. Dave was a big help in that regard.

Clarke was soon at the site of the first robbery, the branch on 42nd Street, now in the guise of a local newspaper reporter—a ruse he used quite often and to good effect to get into crime scenes and talk to witnesses to gather information. He was seated with the branch manager, a portly, overly stuffy old fellow named Caruthers, when the news of the recent robbery at the Lexington Avenue branch was once more broadcast over the radio in his office. Hearing the news over the radio really got the manager upset. Clarke noted the report added that it was not only the safety deposit box of wealthy socialite Mrs. Van Camp that had been broken into, but all the boxes in the branch. It was astounding to Caruthers, but Clarke just nodded: facts were falling into place.

"My God!" Caruthers gasped, indignant with anger and alarm. "Another robbery? This is terrible!"

Bob Clarke gave an imperceptible nod of his head at the recent turn of events. "The second bank in two days and both are Security National branches."

"Yes, oh my, this is terrible! Terrible, I tell you! I hope no one was hurt," Caruthers added nervously, almost as an afterthought. Clarke could see that the man's true concern was with the wealth that had been stolen. It was obvious he felt that his branch of the bank was invulnerable, impervious to any such robbery or that sort of thing. Now he was shocked, unnerved by the thefts and the vast amounts stolen.

Bob Clarke wanted to get over to the Lexington Avenue branch as soon as possible, but first he needed to finish with Caruthers here and examine the vault system at this location.

"So tell me, Mr. Caruthers, exactly how is the vault system set up?"

"The vault is in the back of the building, a timed lock of course, set to open precisely at 9 a.m., and then locked shut the previous evening at precisely 5 p.m. No one can get inside. Inside is the bank safe—where we keep the cash and securities that make up the bulk of our holdings—that is always locked and can not be opened without my special key. I have the only one. The interesting thing, Mr. Clarke, is that the bank safe was never touched, only the safety deposit boxes that line the corner of the far wall of the vault."

"Can I see the vault now?" Clarke asked.

"Of course, I'll take you there myself," Caruthers replied, lifting his massive bulk out of his chair with a huff. He then led his guest to the back of the building, through a security gate, through the open vault door and then into the vault itself.

Clarke examined the large room carefully. Nothing seemed out of order. "The police were here?"

"Of course," Caruthers replied with a sigh. "Inspector Blaine and his men."

"What did they say about this?"

Caruthers shrugged, "What could they say? They found nothing. Of course they noticed the rifled safety deposit boxes but the job was done so cleanly they could find no evidence. I had no idea that the boxes had been breached at all myself."

Clarke nodded, it fit the M.O. of this particular robber so far—whoever he might be. The criminal was a very cagey and slick operator; he did not draw attention to himself or his actions and then seemingly disappeared without a trace. Perhaps the papers were correct in dubbing him 'The Mystery Man.'

Bob Clarke looked over the large room that made up the Security National Bank vault. It was made of thick grey steel and contained two large secure bank safes that were locked shut. This was where the bank kept its considerable cash reserves and millions of dollars worth of bearer bonds. and yet it had remained untouched. The thieves seemingly had no interest with these safes even allowing for the vast wealth within them. That fact perplexed the young investigator at first.

"I just don't understand why the robbers went for the boxes and not the safes," Caruthers said anxiously, stating the obvious, and putting words to Clarke's own thoughts. "We have a lot of cash stored in those safes. Hundreds of thousands of dollars in cash at any moment. From a criminal point of view, it does not seem to make much sense for them not to even attempt to open those safes."

"No, actually, it does make sense. Perfect sense. The robbers—and I'm beginning to believe we are looking for only one very bold and cunning fellow—did not have the equipment to open these massive bank safes. I think your robber was one man, and he would need a heavy-duty drill and explosives to breach these kinds of safes. He did not have that kind of large and heavy equipment and he could not bring it in here with him unnoticed. But he did have with him enough small picks and chisels, perhaps in a briefcase, to force open the much less secure doors to the safety deposit boxes. Those are far easier to open and rifle given all the time he had."

"But he'd need many hours," Caruthers said boldly.

"Unless I miss my guess, Mr. Caruthers, your thief had all the time he needed—he had all night," Clarke added confidently.

"Well, I don't know about that, Mr. Clarke," Caruthers said sharply. "The police certainly seem baffled. I imagine the disaster here in my branch is old news by now and that they are all at the Lexington branch seeking clues."

"I'm sure they are, Mr. Caruthers, and I am planning on stopping there soon," Clarke added as his eyes scanned the safety deposit boxes once again, noting exactly how they were set up. He eyed them suspiciously, carefully. The boxes themselves were roughly three inches high by six inches wide, with each box having a door with a key lock and a number on the outside of it. There were two sections of boxes, five feet high and twelve feet long, the sections set in a corner perpendicular to each other. On first glance, they all appeared untouched, the doors closed, apparently locked and not disturbed. There was no debris in evidence, no empty boxes strewn across the vault floor, or any papers or money thrown about.

"A very neat job, indeed."

"Too neatly done for my taste, Mr. Clarke. Why, I didn't even realize there had been a robbery until many hours after the bank opened yesterday," Caruthers muttered regretfully.

"And that's exactly what your thief had in mind," Clarke told the bank manager, then he took one last look at the two rows of rifled boxes, then at the locked bank safes and nodded knowingly. "Your robber, this so-called 'Mystery Man,' seems to have intended for his theft not to be discovered right away. That is separate and aside from the obvious reasons of not wanting to be discovered so as to allow him to make his getaway. I wonder why?"

"Well, I can see he did not want it discovered right away," Caruthers blurted in frustration. "The man is a fiend, a diabolical fiend."

"Perhaps," Clarke allowed. "Perhaps he has other reasons for his actions."

"What other reasons?" the manager asked, stunned.

Bob Clarke smiled grimly, "Well, that's all for now, Mr. Caruthers. I must go. Thank you for your help."

"Ah, what newspaper did you say you were from?" Caruthers asked curiously.

"Oh, did I say I was from a newspaper? I'm a freelance reporter," Clarke explained with a slim smile as he left the bank, leaving Caruthers standing alone with a large blank stare.

Clarke then quickly exited the bank on the 42nd Street side where he walked towards a waiting roadster. Behind the wheel was the lovely grey-eyed beauty, Sandra Gray, and after he got into the car she immediately put it in gear and took off flowing into the heavy Manhattan traffic.

"I got here as soon as I could, Bob," Sandy told her friend, who was also the man she loved. "So what do you think?"

"I think we're up against a very cagey crook," Clarke replied, as his sharp mind ran over the various facts and features of the crime.

"How is he pulling off these robberies? I mean, the papers say there was no evidence of forced entrance into the vaults of both bank branches, nor the banks themselves," Sandy asked. She quickly changed gear and headed down 42nd Street and then over to Lexington Avenue.

"That's true, Sandy," Clarke told her as he thought over what he had just learned. He noticed she drove her roadster like a pro race car driver, better than any New York cabbie could do, weaving in and out of the confusing Manhattan traffic. "I have a theory, but I'll have to see the layout of the vault in the Lexington Avenue branch first."

"Okay, Bob, I'll have you there in two minutes. Well, maybe three in this traffic," she smiled, gunning the roadster around a stopped delivery truck that was blocking everyone. She swung around the truck onto the sidewalk and then hung a hard right onto Lexington Avenue. Sandy got Bob to the bank branch in under three minutes. The cops were still there. Sandy pulled the roadster over to the curb, parked.

Clarke looked over at Sandy with a thankful nod for the ride, then before he got out of the car he told her, "Whoever is doing these robberies is making off with a lot of jewelry, that means he needs a serious fence to dispose of all the hot loot. I want you to go and speak with a guy I know over in Brooklyn, name of Sammy Bolt. He's done some fencing over the years. He tells me he's gone straight now, but he still owes me a favor. He runs a pawn shop on Gold Street, right around the corner from the local precinct house. See what Bolt has to say; maybe he's heard something on the grapevine about hot gems coming on the market."

"Will do, Bob. What about you?" Sandy asked.

"The Crimson Mask is going banking," Clarke said simply, offering her a meaningful smile as he opened the car door.

Sandy grabbed his arm and held him back, then gave him a sly look, "You okay, you sure you're not getting too old for this?"

Clarke offered her a boyish grin, "Don't worry; I'll let you know when I'm ready to retire."

Sandy nodded back, then watched the man she loved exit the vehicle and walk towards the bank entrance. Afterwards she pulled her sleek roadster away from the curb and headed to Brooklyn.

Before he entered the bank Bob Clarke found a moment when no one was around and surreptitiously slipped on his red velvet domino mask to suddenly become the ace crime fighter—the Crimson Mask. People coming out of the bank through the revolving doors saw him in the red mask and stared in awe. Some smiled or nodded, glad to see that the heroic crime fighter was now on the case. Others turned away in fear at the sight of the mysterious masked man in their midst.

Inside the bank Clarke saw Police Inspector Blaine and walked on over to the large, old-school copper. "Hello, Blaine, so how does it look?"

"Oh, you! The Crimson Mask himself!" Blaine replied looking intently at the masked man who now stood before him. The Crimson Mask wore a black suit, dark tie, crepe-soled shoes and a red velvet domino mask that effectively hid his identity.

Blaine nodded. He was a big, gruff copper, a long-time detective whose bull-headed tenacity had paid off and effectively got him promoted to Inspector. Now he was given the tough problems, the perplexing mysteries, like this 'Mystery Man' case. He had worked with the Crimson Mask over the last few months and was not too proud to take whatever help he could get from the man. He was always relieved when he saw the Crimson Mask on a case because the masked man—whoever he might be—had an uncanny ability to solve crimes.

Inspector Blaine had also known Bob Clarke's slain father from the old days—but Blaine did not know his slain friend's son was the masked crime fighter. He did know the Crimson Mask was obsessed with fighting crime and with that in mind he always tried to help the police. So Blaine had grown to value the masked man's judgment and advice. Blaine was also a cop whom the Crimson Mask often called offering interesting theories or hints about difficult to solve crimes that always seemed to pay off. Blaine was a man who knew it was best for a cop to always keep his ear to the ground and listen to any tips that could be used to solve a case, and when the Crimson Mask was on a case that meant it was big!

"I have to tell you we're stumped on this one," Blaine admitted reluctantly, openly showing a sense of defeat that was not his usual response to any criminal case. "The bank doors, nor the vault itself show any sign of forced entry or tampering. No possible way to enter the vault. No apparent damage at all. And they didn't even touch the bank safes inside the vault. There was big money in them and they didn't even make a try for 'em—just like at the other branch yesterday. It has us baffled."

"Not they, Inspector, but he. I am sure you're looking for just one robber, but a very bold and cunning fellow. It is only one man, not a gang. Of that I am certain," Clarke stated.

Blaine nodded, "Makes sense, I guess. So he passed by the safes and went directly to the boxes. Why?"

"Easy money, fast money, a simple quick job. It makes sense," Clarke offered.

"I guess you're right," Blaine admitted. "There was a load of jewels there. What I want to know is how did he get in and steal everything without anyone seeing him?"

"Let's take a look at that vault. You don't mind, do you?" the Crimson Mask asked the police inspector. It was more as a curtesey, one which Blaine appreciated. "I'll follow you."

Blaine shrugged, "Sure, come on, I'll take you there myself. The fingerprints boys must be done by now anyway, but I don't expect we'll get any good prints on this case. They'll find a lot of them of course—but all from bank employees or every customer who ever rented a box—but not these guys—or this guy—as you say."

The Crimson Mask nodded. He assumed that the thief had to be a box renter, one who must have signed a card to obtain the box originally so he could have access to the vault and the box section in the first place. But there were hundreds of names and Clarke knew that the name they were looking for would most likely be fictitious with a phony address. No help there.

The Crimson Mask allowed himself to be shown into the vault by the Inspector. He knew the man they were looking for seemed to be a professional with some special knowledge—a smart guy like this would be sure to wear gloves and not leave behind any fingerprints or other evidence. So checking for any prints was a colossal waste of police time—but the grunt work still had to be done. The cops still had to go through the motions and hope something came up. Clarke was not at all hopeful in that regard.

"Here it is," Blaine said, leading the masked man through the massive time-locked steel door to the large grey metal-walled room that made up the bank vault.

Immediately Bob Clarke noticed one very interesting thing—it looked just like the vault at the 42nd Street branch. Across one wall were various locked cabinets and then two large carbon steel safes, locked shut. Once again, these bank safes inside the vault had remained untouched by the robber. Across the far wall were two rows of safety deposit boxes, once again they were in two sections that were set perpendicular to each other over in the corner.

"So what do you make of it?" Blaine asked hopefully.

"Looks like the same set-up as the vault at the 42nd Street branch," Clarke noted.

"It is. I asked the manager here about that, and he told me all National Security branches are designed to very strict specifications to ensure total security. Or anyway, that's what he told me and that's the way things had been until now. The company spiel. It's not so secure now, is it?"

"No," the Crimson Mask admitted softly, now in deep thought as he roamed around the vault, looking over the room with a practiced investigatory eye. Suddenly he smiled knowingly. He had noticed something of interest. He immediately walked over to the far corner of the vault and focused upon the rows of safety deposit boxes there. They appeared to be undamaged but each one had in fact been carefully broken into and rifled of its contents, just as at the other branch. Then the box had been carefully put back inside the slot and the door shut. This had been done with each box in this branch—just as it had been done at the previous bank branch—no litter or stray dollar bills left on the floor, nothing to indicate at first glance that a robbery had even taken place at all.

"Very clean job," the masked man stated simply.

"Yes, a pro job, to be sure," the Inspector added.

The Crimson Mask wasn't so sure about that last part just yet. "Blaine,

"So what do you make of it?"

call in the manager, I have some questions for him," Clarke stated tersely from behind his mask, almost as if he was in some form of trance, for he would not allow himself to take his eyes off those rows of boxes for one moment.

"You see something?" Blaine asked hopefully.

"Not sure yet, just bring the manager here."

Inspector Blaine left the vault to get the manager.

Now, the Crimson Mask was finally alone inside the vault. He quickly examined the corner area that had caught his interest. It was a place where the two sections of boxes met perpendicular to each other. There was a slim plywood covering over that corner, painted to blend in with the color of the box section. It was just for show. Bob Clarke reached up and removed the covering and discovered an opening in the corner created by the two perpendicular rows of boxes.

The Crimson Mask nodded as he looked down into what was a small open triangular area. It was certainly large enough for a man to hide in. Clarke took out his flashlight and ran it over the opening, at the bottom of which he saw what appeared to be an empty candy wrapper and an empty soda bottle—evidence of the Mystery Man for sure. Clarke smiled at his discovery. This was significant. Then he quickly set the covering back in place and walked away from the box section and over towards one of the steel safes. Soon Blaine got back with a Mr. Miles Stanhope, the branch manager and a man by all accounts who was impatience personified. Blaine introduced the banker to the Crimson Mask. The bank manager hardly knew what to say to the mysterious masked figure standing there in his vault.

"The Crimson Mask assists the police sometimes," Blaine explained simply. "He has graciously agreed to help in this case."

"I see. All right, so you wanted to see me?" Stanhope blurted, looking with evident surprise and some awe at the masked man standing there in front of him. He wondered just what the police hoped to gain by allowing such a fellow on this case. Stanhope sighed; he was a very busy man right now, a man who did not like to be questioned by masked men about intimate bank matters.

"Nothing too serious, Mr. Stanhope," the Crimson Mask said simply. "I'll not keep you long. I just wanted to confirm something Inspector Blaine mentioned."

"And what would that be?"

"That this vault, and the one at your other branch on 42nd Street that was robbed yesterday—they seem to have very similar designs."

Stanhope nodded proudly, "Of course, but not similar, they are identical. These are identical designs. Security National Bank is a leader in secure banking and we take it as a matter of great pride that our bank vaults have never been broken into or robbed …"

"Until now," the masked man reminded him sharply.

Stanhope reddened but ignored the remark, instead adding, "We take our security and the security of our customers very seriously, I can assure you."

"I'm sure that you do," the Crimson Mask stated in a clipped tone. He looked at Blaine and then back at Stanhope. "Tell me, Mr. Stanhope, do you mean to tell me that the design of your vault system in the two banks that have been robbed is identical?"

"Yes, they are all identical," Stanhope replied a bit tartly, showing his impatience.

The Crimson Mask looked over at the man's face and an annoyed grimace played across his lips. "I want to be clear on exactly what you are telling me. Are you also saying that all your branches in the Security National chain have this identical vault design?"

"Yes, of course," Stanhope blurted with ill-concealed impatience. "They are all the same. They were designed that way for security purposes, no doubt … Now I really must get back to my desk. This robbery is terrible for business and requires my personal attention to calm irate customers. I need to keep their savings and business accounts within this bank. It is not an easy task under the circumstances. Now may I get back to work? And can you allow Inspector Blaine here to catch these damnable thieves as soon as possible."

"Thief," the Crimson Mask corrected the banker. "It was only one thief."

Stanhope digested that for a moment, then replied, "That's impossible. It was most certainly the work of some professional gang to do all that was done here. We have over one thousand safety deposit boxes and they hit them all!"

The Crimson Mask stated simply, "This theft was done by only one very bold man and he did it all himself. Alone. All in one night."

"That's impossible!" Stanhope barked. "Inspector?"

Blaine looked at the masked man thoughtfully, "You seem very sure about this."

"Yes, I am sure it was only one man, Inspector."

Inspector Blaine looked at the banker, "That's good enough for me, Mr. Stanhope."

"Blah! I can not put up with all this now. Robbers—police—masked men! It is just too much. I have irate customers on my back clamoring to have their stolen jewelry returned. What do I tell them? We are talking about a million dollars in gems, gentlemen. Mr. Lowe, the bank president, is nearly apoplectic with alarm over these robberies. What do I tell him and my customers, Inspector? When will an arrest be made and the stolen items returned?"

Blaine sighed deeply, "We are working on it, Mr. Stanhope, we are working on it."

The bank manager growled with frustration then walked briskly out of the vault in a mad huff. Clarke sympathized with the man's problems, but he had a crime to solve and a thief to catch and no time for the manager's alarmed hysterics.

Now Inspector Blaine and the Crimson Mask were alone.

"So," Blaine asked carefully, "what have you discovered?"

The Crimson Mask looked at Inspector Blaine and nodded, "You have a complex case on your hands. It will take some explaining."

"Well, I'm here now and I'm ready to hear it," Blaine insisted.

A sleek roadster crossed over the Manhattan Bridge into Brooklyn. The young blonde driving the vehicle wove in and out of traffic like a pro, quickly driving down Flastbush Avenue, hanging a right onto Gold Street, passing the precinct house and then over to number 147, the pawn shop run by Sammy Bolt.

Sandy Gray parked her small roadster at the curb under the three hanging globes that indicated a pawnbroker's establishment. Sandy remained in her car and looked over the place first, noticing that it seemed old and dirty, the windows streaked with soot and grime, but it was loaded with an odd assortment of interesting items. And business seemed to be brisk. She saw people bringing in items to pawn, while others walked out with cash or goods they had just purchased or redeemed.

Sandy continued to watch the place for a few more minutes before she got out of her car and then walked towards the store. She looked into the store and noticed a large amount of musical instruments, fancy clothing including hundred-dollar suits, books, statues, household items, and of course a large assortment of jewelry in the store window and a long row of showcases. Jewelry was her target on this particular visit. As she entered the shop a tiny bell on the door tinkled, letting the man inside know that another sucker—er…customer—had come into his shop.

The guy behind the counter was old and overweight and was arguing with a younger man about just how much money he deserved for pawning his beloved clarinet. The youngster appeared to be just another jazz musician on hard times or strapped for cash to buy dope. However, when the owner saw the pretty petite blonde that had just entered his shop he quickly gave the guy with whom he'd been talking the bum's rush and had him out the door in a flash.

"Be gone now, Mousey. Come back later when I'm not so busy," the owner growled as he chased the young man away and out the door. The young man was obviously a local hophead in need of a fix. The owner knew he could wait for what he needed. The lovely young woman who had just entered his store could not. When the musician was gone the owner turned his full attention on the attractive young blonde and she was well worth the look. Bolt glued his roving eyes towards the petite form of the lovely young woman walking towards him and gave her his best toothy smile, "And what can I do for you today, Young Miss?"

Sandra Gray walked over towards the counter, taking in the full measure of the man before her. She didn't really like what she saw at first. But if Bob Clarke thought this guy had gone straight—well, he might be true, but he sure didn't look that way to her. She certainly didn't trust the man by the looks of him. But Sandy knew looks could be deceiving.

Sandy gave him her most winning smile, "Hello, I'm Sandra Gray. Are you Sammy Bolt?"

"Yes, mam, the one and only, at your service."

"Well, a friend of mine referred me to you as the person who would have the bead on stolen jewelry in this city."

The man suddenly froze, now suspicious of the young woman in front of him. She didn't look like any cop he'd ever seen before. "Do I know you? I don't think I know you."

"No," Sandy replied carefully, "but you know my friend and you owe him a favor and he sent me here to collect."

Sammy looked alarmed, slowly reaching for something behind the counter but he did not bring it out yet. "And who might your friend be, Missy?"

Sandy smiled sweetly, her hand was already in her purse and her finger rested on the trigger of her .38 should she need to withdraw the weapon and use it. Sammy's movement towards some weapon behind the counter had not been missed by her.

Sandy moved closer to the counter, put her index finger to her luscious red lips to indicate discretion, then crooked her finger calling Sammy even closer.

Sammy Bolt nodded, smiled and moved closer, not scared of this slip of a gal, but he did want to hear what this bold young woman had to say. He was nervous, maybe fearful; a mug never knew who he was really dealing with these days, but he had to know who had sent her. He was surprised when she whispered just three words, "the Crimson Mask."

Sammy looked closely at the blonde and just nodded. He recognized the name and it sent a shiver through him. If the masked man had sent her here that was an entirely different kettle of fish. He said, "Wait one minute."

Sammy stepped out from behind the counter over to the front door, put out the 'Closed' sign on a hook and then locked the door. Then he came back to the counter and the mysterious young woman who waited so patiently.

"Okay, you're right. I do owe him a favor, and one thing Sammy Bolt always does is pay his debts," the man said simply. He smiled almost wickedly. "So what do you want to know?"

"You have your ear to what's going on in the fencing of stolen jewelry…" Sandy stated quickly.

"Now wait—I don't do that any more. I'm done with all that! I've gone straight, strictly legit now. And I know what you're after if you work for him—that masked man! You think I might be involved in those Security National Bank robberies I've read about in the newspapers? Well, I'm not! Not these days. Was a time once, years back when I might ha' been tempted, but not today, Missy. My fencing days is over."

"That's good to hear, Mr. Bolt. Honesty is always the best policy," Sandy said with her winning smile. She didn't want to antagonize the man; she wanted to get him to cooperate, to talk. To spill.

Bolt grimaced, as though he had swallowed a particularly large or distasteful pill.

"I'm sure your new life is much more rewarding and safer than your past criminal one," Sandy offered demurely.

"Not more rewarding, doll, but I can't go back to prison any more. I can't do more time at my age," Sammy said softly. "So what do you want?"

"Not me, our masked friend. He wants to know if anyone has approached you to fence stolen jewelry, maybe break up pieces or cut out the gems for resale? You hear anything about anything like that?

"Noooo…" Bolt said slow, and careful. "Nothing yet, but it's early. The robberies just happened the last couple days. In a situation like this you got basically two scenarios. One, the thieves will try to fence the swag as soon as they can. Usually they'll do that if they need cash fast. Or want cash fast. Two, if they are smart, they could sit on the haul for weeks, months, maybe even years—then you—and your 'friend'—are plum out of luck, sister."

"Well, what about your first scenario? Will you call me if you hear anything along those lines?" Sandy asked in all sweetness.

"Yeah, I can do that. If I hear anything along those lines, I'll call you— for the Mask. I still owe him. Tell him Sammy Bolt always pays his debts."

"I will. Good then, Mr. Bolt," Sandy replied, handing the man a card with her name and a phone number. "I hope to hear from you. Thank you, Mr. Bolt."

"Always willing to help The Mask, Missy. I'll see what I can come up with; I'll ask around, someone's gotta know something. These robberies are top-notch jobs and big news; they'll have a lotta people talking."

"Now unlock this door and let me out of here," Sandy told him. Then she left the pawn shop and got back into her roadster for the drive back into Manhattan.

Meanwhile, back in the vault of the Security National Bank on Lexington Avenue, Police Inspector Blaine and the Crimson Mask were alone in deep conversation.

The masked man led the Inspector to the corner of the vault where the safety deposit boxes were located. He asked the Inspector, "You notice anything peculiar about the set-up of these two rows of boxes?"

Blaine took a closer look at the rows of boxes. The big detective finally shrugged, "No, nothing except the obvious."

The Crimson Mask nodded, "Yes, the obvious. Now we move on to the not so obvious. I'm going to show you something very interesting, Inspector, and when I do I want you to keep in mind what Mr. Stanhope just told us …"

Blaine looked at the masked man before him intently, nodded, then answered as he remembered the words the bank manager had told them moments before, "You mean what he said about all the Security National vaults being identical?"

"Precisely," the Crimson Mask answered sharply. Now the masked man drew the Inspector's attention to the corner created by the perpendicular design of the two rows of boxes. "See here, the two rows meet at this corner."

Blaine nodded, watching the man before him carefully, but he still did not get what he was trying to show him

The Crimson Mask smiled as he suddenly lifted a matching covering over the corner where the two rows met to reveal an open triangular space. An open space created by the two rows of boxes that had been set perpendicular to each other in the corner.

"What the blazes!" Blaine shouted in surprise.

"Big enough for one man to hide in, big enough for our thief."

"Amazing!" Blaine added, his eyes fixated upon the opening.

"Not amazing, what it is, is a serious design flaw in the way the bank has set up the safety deposit boxes. Our thief somehow discovered this and has taken advantage of it. And remember, this flawed design is replicated in every Security National branch in the city," the Crimson Mask added in dire warning.

Blaine looked fearful now, his gaze shifted down into the triangular hole once again, as Clarke handed him a flashlight.

"Look down at the bottom," the masked man told him, "you can see someone has been in there."

"Yes," Blaine answered almost in awe, moving his flashlight to illuminate the space. He had never expected this. "Amazing! This seems perfect for an inside job then."

"Inspector," the Crimson Mask told him, "I believe our thief entered the vault as a bank customer to access his safety deposit box. He carried with him a small briefcase, containing simple burglary tools. When he was alone he pulled back the corner lid and climbed into the hole, then once inside he simply pulled back the lid covering the opening. He was careful to remain quiet until the bank closed. Once the bank closed its doors, he came out of his bolt hole and got to work on the boxes. He worked quietly but quickly all night long. Once done he returned to his bolt hole until the bank vault was opened the next morning. Then, when no one was looking, he exited the hole and calmly walked out of the vault, and the bank, no one the wiser. It would be many minutes—if not some hours—before a customer went into the vault to go to their box, and noticed it had been rifled. Soon the bank would discover that all the boxes had been rifled, but by then our thief was long gone with his loot."

"That's amazing! Truly masterful! The man really is a Mystery Man," Blaine admitted angrily, then his face clouded over with gloom remembering the masked man's words, "But this is very bad for us."

"Do you know how many branches Security National has in the city?" the Crimson Mask asked the Inspector.

"No, I will have to ask Mr. Stanhope, but I am sure they have dozens of branches," Blaine murmured, already thinking things through and seeing the situation was far more complex and serious than he had at first ever believed.

"Good, then speak to Stanhope. You need to get the locations of each of these branches and have one of your men stationed in each branch ready for action when they open the next morning," the Crimson Mask told the Inspector. "Then if our thief makes an appearance we'll catch him."

"I'll do that," Blaine explained.

"You have to have your man at each branch each morning, waiting and ready for action when that vault is opened. Have the manager and your man go straight into the vault and check that bolt hole in the corner. If the thief is hiding in there, you'll have him. Then call in your detectives and make the arrest. The only problem is we have no idea which of the dozens of branches will be next. It could be any one of them. He may not even act tonight, perhaps tomorrow, or days from now, so we have no idea when he will strike next."

"Nor where," Blaine added glumly.

"True, and that's what I'm going to try to discover, Inspector," the masked man said sternly.

Then the Crimson Mask stormed out of the vault walking through the bank towards the exit doors. As he went through the revolving doors, and when no one was looking, he quickly slipped off his red velvet domino mask and once again became regular citizen, Bob Clarke. No one had seen him. Clarke then stood by the doorway and lit a cigarette, thinking over what he had just learned. This was becoming quite the intricate case and he wondered just who this 'Mystery Man' might be.

Clarke heard the car horn, and that got his attention as a sleek roadster pulled up to the curb in front of him. Behind the wheel was the lovely Sandra Gray, all five feet and three inches of her cool Dresden china beauty.

"Hey, Bob, need a ride?" she asked pertly. Sandy was the love of his life and his most trusted agent, she was always right where he needed her to be and always ready to help in his cases.

"Sure, lady," he said lightly as he got into the passenger side of the vehicle, then Sandra took off down Lexington Avenue. "Seems you're back just in time from Brooklyn."

"Yes, and that Sammy Bolt fellow is a real character, but I think he will let us know if he hears about anyone fencing a large amount of stolen jewelry."

"Good. Now let's head on back to the store, Dave must be boiling over with jealousy that we were out all day having all the fun and left him to work the counter."

"Dave can handle it," Sandy laughed sweetly, gunning the little roadster downtown and towards the East Side where Bob Clarke had his drug store and the Crimson Mask had his secret headquarters.

They were seated in the hidden room in the back of the drug store on the corner of East Avenue and Carmody Street. Dave Small had put a 'Closed' sign on the front door and locked it to keep out any interruption from a stray customer while Bob and his trio discussed the Security National Bank robberies.

Behind the steel-grey door that led to Clarke's secret room was a modern laboratory crammed with the most up-to-date apparatus for the scientific detection of crime. With him now were Sandra, his assistant Dave, and also former Police Commissioner Theodore Warrick. Warrick, an older man of 60 years in age, began the conversation.

"Well, Bob, I'm glad to hear that the Crimson Mask is on this case. It seems to be a very complicated robbery scheme. After what you described to us about the design flaw in the vaults, there could be many more robberies before we catch this so-called 'Mystery Man'".

"I'm sure he's taking down a branch somewhere this very night even as we are here talking," Clarke said in obvious frustration. He had no idea where the thief would strike next and had to rely on Blaine's men staked out at each branch to report to him in the morning.

"Yeah, Boss, but which one?" Dave Small chimed in.

"That's the problem," Clarke replied grimly. He hated this waiting for news; he wanted to see action and catch the bad guy right away. It was the only reason he had become the Crimson Mask and begun his one-man fight against crime in the first place. That, and to avenge his slain father. But Bob Clarke knew he had to be patient in this game, work the crime and the criminal smartly, then he could catch the man.

Clarke sighed deeply, hating the feeling of helplessness that surrounded him now. "Inspector Blaine has his men stationed at each bank branch. In the morning when the timed vaults open at 9 a.m., they're bound to catch the intruder at one of these branches, then we'll have our thief and put him behind bars where he belongs. Or so I hope. It's just a matter of being patient; waiting for the robber to act, and then Blaine's men will get him."

"So you're waiting for a call, Boss?" Dave asked.

"Yes, but it won't come for many hours from now, so there's nothing we can do until then. You can all go home now, get some sleep. We'll meet here tomorrow morning precisely at 8 a.m.," Clarke told Dave and Sandy. He looked over to Ted Warrick, the older man looked done in. "Ted, why don't you go home, too. No need for you to be here in the morning. I'll call you later and let you know what happened after the banks open."

Ted Warrick nodded, gave his friend a reassuring pat on the shoulder, "I'm sure the Crimson Mask has everything well in hand."

The next morning Dave Small opened the drug store on the Lower East Side at 8 a.m. and soon Sandra Gray came by. Then the two stepped into the back room where Bob Clarke—affectionately known by the neighborhood folk as Doc Clarke—was already busy with a large wall map of the city that showed dozens of Security National Bank branches.

Each bank branch was indicated on the map with a red pin and there seemed to be almost one-hundred pins stuck into the map throughout Manhattan.

"I had no idea there were so many bank branches," Sandy said, as she eyed the map with alarm. "Good morning, Bob."

"Good morning, Sandy. Now you can see what we're up against. Right now I'm waiting for the call from Inspector Blaine," Clarke replied, fidgeting as he added new pins into locations across the river in Brooklyn from another list of branches in that borough. "There's no guarantee our robber will even stick to Manhattan. He may go over the bridge to a Brooklyn branch."

"Well that complicates things," Sandy added.

Clarke nodded, but he gave Sandy a bright smile, she looked so lovely in the morning. She was a sight to behold.

"You think Blaine will come through, Boss?" Dave asked curiously.

"Yes, I'm sure the man we are looking for has been up to no good in one of those branches overnight, and once that vault is open and checked, we'll have him caught red-handed."

"That's good, Boss," Dave replied. "So we just wait for Blaine's call?"

"Yes, but this waiting is killing me," Clarke admitted with frustration.

"Well, it's almost 9 a.m. now, Bob," Sandy said in anticipation, then thoughtfully added, "but you have to give Blaine some time to coordinate things. I figure it shouldn't be much after 9 o'clock until we hear something certain. I'd guess by 9:30, latest."

"That sounds about right," Clarke admitted.

"Of course, I'm still holding out on the hope to hear something from your pawn shop guy, Sammy Bolt," Sandy added quickly. "He told me he'd keep his ears open and I gave him the special phone number here."

"Good work, maybe Sammy will come through with a lead," Clarke said hopefully, his impatience growing with the tick-tock of the large clock overhead. It was now 9 a.m., and Bob knew he should be hearing from Blaine at any moment. The anticipation was killing him.

The minutes wore on.

Time passed.

Dave Small looked at the clock overhead, sighed deeply, then looked over towards Sandra Gray. She just nodded, didn't say a word to Bob, not wanting to upset the man she loved. Meanwhile, Bob Clarke sat still in deep thought, thinking of his slain father and hoping against hope that this latest case would result in the capture of this dangerous criminal, he hoped would soon see the inside of a prison cell for many years.

Clarke tried to remain calm but he couldn't ignore the constant and cloying ticking of the clock overhead; he felt like taking it down from the wall and smashing it to bits on the floor. Instead he reluctantly looked up at the timepiece, noticed where the hands were located and sighed with alarm, "It's almost 10 a.m.. Something has gone wrong."

Sandy nodded at his words but did not know what to say.

Dave Small offered up the only thing he could think of, "You want me to put in a call to Inspector Blaine for you, Boss?"

"No, not yet, Dave. He's at headquarters at One Police Plaza waiting himself for his men to call in, just as we are waiting for him," Clarke said softly. "We'll hold on for a few more minutes."

That annoying clock above them on the wall suddenly struck 10 a.m. Instantly the telephone rang loudly as all three of the people there jumped up, startled like a spring releasing wound up stress. Sandy and Dave allowed a nervous laugh over the tension; Bob Clarke reached over and quickly picked up the special phone.

"Yes?" Clarke asked sharply. This was the special back room phone line used only for crime fighting work. It was not part of the drug store outside this secret room.

"This is Blaine," a gruff voice came over the receiver.

"Yes, I've been waiting to hear from you," Bob Clarke said in a mysterious tone. "This is the Crimson Mask."

"Yes, sorry I'm late, we have a problem," Blaine said seriously. "It seems this thief has some accomplices. Quiet a few of them, in fact. I don't know fully all of what happened last night yet, but I've received reports that many bank branches have discovered men hidden in the vaults. This was something I never expected. The men were all discovered inside when the vaults were opened at 9 a.m. My men caught two of the men but others got away. One of my policemen was wounded and one of the robbers was killed in a gunfight. It seems you were as right as you were wrong on this case. There was a gang after all. It'll get back to you when I learn more. We're still coordinating reports from our men out in the field here at HQ, there may be other branches affected. I'll contact you once I learn more."

Bob Clarke was devastated. He slowly put down the phone as if in a trance. How could he have been so wrong about this case? What had he missed? He was surprised and bitter with anger at his own obvious error.

"What is it, Boss?" Dave asked with growing concern, noticing the grave look on his friend's face.

"Bob?" Sandy called out carefully, nervousness now. "What is it?"

Clarke didn't want to talk about his mistake, but he knew that Dave and Sandy deserved to know the truth of what had happened. He told them what Blaine had just said. Clarke added, "I was so certain this was a single thief, bold and cunning certainly, but a lone-wolf. Now it looks like I was wrong, and that it was in fact, some gang. I still don't believe it. The police have two men captured and are bringing them in to a holding cell at headquarters. They are the key. The Crimson Mask must question them immediately."

"What do you want us to do, Boss?" Dave asked quickly.

"Dave, you're going to kill me, but I want you to stay here and cover the store. I know you want to get in on the action and you will, I promise, but for now I need to keep things appearing normal here. You understand. I can't keep closing the store every time I'm out on a case."

Dave Small reluctantly nodded. He would help his friend and mentor any way he was able.

Suddenly the telephone rang again. Clarke grasped it like a lifeline, wondering just what else Blaine had discovered. Only it wasn't the Inspector at the other end of the line this time, it was the pawnbroker, Sammy Bolt.

"Sammy?" Clarke asked with surprise but interest.

"That's me. Are you—is this—you know…? The Crimson Mask?"

"I am the Crimson Mask," Clarke was able to say in a mysterious and

"Yes, I've been waiting to hear from you."

yet powerful voice.

Sandy smiled, picturing the wily pawnbroker in nervous awe with the realization that he was in fact speaking to the famed crime fighter.

"Wow!" the voice at the other end said in a gruff whisper.

"Do you have news for me?" Clarke asked impatiently, allowing a slight grin to play across his lips as he looked towards Sandy. It appeared her work might yet yield some results.

"Do I!" Bolt blurted seriously. "I got news you'd never imagine. I got news this bank vault thief—that 'Mystery Man'—has been working a crime operation all along."

Bob Clarke was sharply alert now, "Tell me about it, Sammy."

"Well, I found out—from some sources I can not mention—you understand…?"

"Yes. Tell me what you discovered," Clarke insisted.

"Well, I found out he did the two robberies just for show. See, he knew they'd make a big splash in the newspapers … Then he sold the idea and plans to other thieves here in town. Each one of them bought in on the plan for $100,000 cash. He took on ten guys, all pro crooks, and he collected a cool million bucks!"

Clarke whistled, "So that's it! A franchise deal. Very bold, very innovative."

Sammy Bolt continued, "Yep, he had a neat plan, I tell you. The thieves were told about the first two robberies in advance, and once it made the papers, they all wanted in on the scheme. It seemed a sure thing."

"And what of this planner? This 'Mystery Man,' do you know who he is, Sammy?"

"Nah, he's smart, I tell you, he lays low. I only heard this from one of the guys he picked as one of his ten crooks, a bosom-buddy of mine from the old days. Ah… I told that pretty blonde I'd call if I heard any news, and I did. I kept my word."

"Thank you, Sammy," Clarke said.

"Well, I hope she's …"

"And she thanks you too, Sammy," Clarke added quickly with a wry grin at Sandy, then he hung up the phone and explained to Dave and Sandy what Sammy had just told him.

"This changes everything, Boss," Dave ventured.

Bob Clarke nodded thoughtfully, "Yes and no. We still continue with our plan as before. We have to track down the man behind all of this—this original Mystery Man. Dave, you stay here at the store. Sandy, I want you to drop by Sammy Bolt, use your feminine wiles on him; I think he may know more than he's told me about this. Work on him. Find out who his contact is and if he will talk, we need someone to spill on just who this Mystery Man is."

"What about you, Boss?" Dave asked.

"Well, I think it is time that the Crimson Mask visited those two police prisoners to see just what can be learned from them. We'll meet back here at noon and compare notes—have Ted meet us here also—then I hope to catch this thief and close the case before midnight."

Inspector Thomas Blaine looked at the man seated across from his desk at police headquarters, "It's most unusual."

"I'm sure it is, but we have an unusual case and we don't have time to waste," the man in the red velvet domino mask replied in earnest.

"All right. I am having them brought up here now," Blaine told the masked crime fighter who went by the name of the Crimson Mask. "There are only two of them that we caught. We identified them as Barney Rouse and Stanley Peach, both with long records as thieves, con men, sometimes second-story men. They're aces at what they do. Your master thief chose his men well."

"So there were ten bank branches with a man discovered in the vaults of each one this morning?"

"Yes," Blaine explained in frustration. "It certainly threw me for a loop at first, especially after what you told me yesterday."

"Me too," the Crimson Mask admitted grimly.

"So what now?" Blaine asked.

"It's the original robber that I want, the planner of all this, the leader. He's the brains behind this, the smart guy who noticed the design flaw in the bank vaults and exploited it. He's the man who sold the plan to ten other thieves, who then, following his master plan, committed more crimes. Only they didn't know we were onto them and that your men were already in the banks waiting for them. If your men had not been there, they would have each gotten away free and easy."

"If you hadn't clued me onto the scheme my men would never have been there to catch them in the first place," Blaine said thankfully.

The Crimson Mask nodded, "So you were only able to catch two of them?'

"Only two," Blaine admitted with disdain. "Two more were killed in shoot outs with my men, another of my men was wounded. The other six thieves are still at large."

"I'm sure you'll pick them up soon enough. I have someone working on that angle now and if these two fellows don't talk, we may get what we need from this other source," the Crimson Mask told him calmly.

"Mind telling me who that 'other' source is?" Blaine asked the man in the red domino mask.

"Yes, I do, for now," Clarke answered tersely. "He may not even have to be brought into this if I find what I need here and now from the two men you have arrested. My guy's trying to go straight—I don't want to nix his future by having him labeled as an informant. A snitch. Not yet."

Blaine nodded, he knew the deal, some old ex-con who didn't want to head back into stir so he was walking the straight and narrow. Maybe.

"Well then, how about you being straight with me? How about you taking off that red mask now and allowing me to know your true identity? It will remain our secret but it would sure go a long way to fostering trust between us," Blaine asked his mysterious guest.

"Are you serious?" the man in the domino mask asked.

"Yes."

"I can't do that," the Crimson Mask replied sternly.

"Can't or won't?" Blaine insisted.

"Well, I can—but then I'd have to kill you!" the man behind the mask replied in a stark voice that seemed deadly serious.

"You're kidding, right?" Blaine asked with a bit of concern having crept into his voice.

The Crimson Mask didn't say a word for a long moment, then he slowly answered, "Yes, Inspector, I am kidding."

Blaine let out a deep breath. "All right, point taken. Keep your secret identity to yourself as you wish, just so long as you help me on this case."

"Thank you, Inspector."

"No, thank you, it was your sharp eyes that caught the design flaw in the vault. Such a thing would never have occurred to me. Your discovery helped us end this entire robbery spree before it really got out of hand. I can't even imagine what the results of it all would be if these additional robbers had gotten away with their heists."

The Crimson Mask nodded, then he rose out of his seat and left the Inspector's office. He walked across the hall to Interview Room A and the man who awaited him there.

Barney Rouse sat fuming in rage, cuffed to a table at police headquarters in the interview room. He couldn't believe his bad fortune. Here he was nabbed by coppers on a sweet bank job that should have been a sure-thing. It was galling. Here he'd paid out a cool one-hundred Gs to the newspaper's Mystery Man, which had been put up for him by a local bookie pending substantial payback and a cut from his safety deposit take. It had been touted as a sure-thing and it looked to be on the up and up. A sure-thing until the Crimson Mask became involved. Barney Rouse cursed the police, he cursed the Mystery Man and he cursed the Crimson Mask.

Then the door to the small holding room opened and the Crimson Mask himself walked into the room. Rouse stared in surprise and awe. He noticed the ace crime fighter was dressed in a black suit, dark tie, crepe-soled shoes and he wore a red velvet domino mask upon his face to hide his identity. Rouse gulped hard in utter terror and sat frozen as he watched the grim visage of the mysterious masked man close the door to the room and then walk closer to him. The Crimson Mask pulled up a chair and sat down at the table opposite the thief looking intently into his eyes—who was now trembling with fear.

"Who are you? What do you want?" Rouse stammered.

"You know who I am, Barney Rouse," the man in the red mask shot back sternly. "I am the Crimson Mask, and I want answers!"

Rouse gulped nervously, "Ah, well, I don't really know nothing ..."

"Your use of a double negative indicates to me that you do know something."

"Eh? I don't know what you're talking about," Rouse said confused now.

Clarke allowed a slim grin, "I want to know what you know about all this."

"I'm telling you the truth," Rouse insisted terrified by the sharp steel grey eyes he saw surrounded by the red velvet mask. Those intent eyes bored down into his own, deep and stark, cold and hard. Rouse gulped nervously, "I'm telling you the truth."

"Who is this Mystery Man?"

"I don't know," Rouse answered, and it sounded sincere.

"Then how were you approached with this scheme?" Clarke demanded.

Rouse shrugged, "Guy calls me, see? Outta the blue, like, but I guess he knows my rep, you know?"

"Go on."

Rouse nodded, he'd already decided to spill what little he knew. He sure as hell didn't owe the Mystery Man any loyalty. That man had sold him a bogus plan that had got him pinched. He'd also gone off and took a hundred grand of his dough. Cash he'd had to borrow to put up for the scheme. Now Rouse was in deep with Bad Joe Montana, a guy you did not want to owe money too—especially money that you no longer had!

"Who did this caller say he was?" the Crimson Mask asked. "What telephone number did he call from, or did he leave you a number to call him back?"

"He told me he was a man who could make me rich. He told me to watch the newspapers the next few days for bank robberies on Monday and Tuesday and that if I liked what I saw and wanted in on the deal to call him back at a certain number at a certain time. I was also told to gather a hundred grand in cash, in small bills, ready to pay him to buy into the sure plan."

"What was the phone number?" Clarke jumped on the question.

"A phone booth on Madison Avenue," Rouse replied with a shrug.

Clarke nodded with obvious disappointment. A phone booth, untraceable now, obviously the other nine thugs had been approached the same way.

"How was the meet set up?" Clarke continued.

Rouse grinned, "Once I read about the sweet robbery in the newspapers, I naturally wanted in on the deal. I wanted my piece, you know? I made the call. I was told to come down to a certain bench in Central Park alone, bring the cash. I'd be given further instructions then."

"So what happened?"

"What happened? I went! I went to the bench under that statue of some Civil War soldier near the park entrance. No one was there. I was alone. I sat down. Waited."

"Then what?"

"Then I heard a voice behind me from within the bushes, it told me not to turn around. I didn't. I knew how these things are usually done. So I went along, I wanted in on the plan. I felt a man come close up behind me, he ordered me again not to turn around or look at him. I didn't. He handed me an envelope with papers in it and told me to look them over. I did."

"You never saw his face?"

"No."

"What was his voice like?"

"Average. I think he was disguising it."

"Go on."

"Well, I looked over the papers and was amazed; it was the real deal, the plans for the perfect heist. Everything was explained in simple black and white. It was so easy. The plans told me exactly what I had to do to pull the plan off successfully. I couldn't believe it. I couldn't believe my good fortune. I handed the man the money and he left. I never saw or heard from him again. That afternoon I entered the bank branch indicated in his plan and did exactly as it told me to do. I thought I was onto a sure-thing! Boy was I wrong! Suddenly everything went to blazes and cops were everywhere! It was supposed to be the perfect heist, but it didn't work!"

"Too bad," the Crimson Mask growled.

"Yeah, too bad for me now."

"Barney, you don't owe this Mystery Man anything. You see the fix he's gotten you into, so think about this now; is there anything else you can tell me about him that can give me a clue to his identity?"

Rouse shrugged, "Nah, I tell you, I never saw him."

Clarke nodded, then a thought occurred to him, "What about when he handed you the plans and took your money?"

Rouse grimaced at the memory, "What about it?"

"Was he wearing gloves?" Clarke insisted.

"Nah, he just … Hey you know …?"

"What is it?"

Barney Rouse looked up into the eyes of the masked man seated across the table from him. "Yeah, you know what? He had no gloves on, but I'll tell you what I did notice, a ring on his right hand. I remember it was a nice bauble, a gold coiled snake ring that was on his right pinky."

The Crimson Mask nodded.

"Does that help you?" Rouse asked hopefully.

"Yes, perhaps it does," Clarke replied softly.

"Then maybe you can put in a good word for me with the coppers?"

"Yes, I will do that, and with the judge too," Clarke said, then the Crimson Mask was gone.

The other thief cooling his heels in Interview Room B was named Stanley Peach, and he was sweating bullets, a jangled mass of raw nerves and bitter anger all rolled up into a sad sack loser looking at jail time once again. Life just wasn't fair.

"How could this happen to me? Me! Stanley Peach, the best thief in the

"…you don't owe the Mystery Man anything."

city! How could I fall for such a sweet deal and then have it all fall apart on me! Now I'm here in lockup and left holding the bag, and I'm down a hundred grand on a scheme that seemed so sweet!"

Peach's monologue was interrupted when the door to the room suddenly burst open and a tall masked man dressed all in black entered.

"You're no cop!" Peach stated nervously.

"And you're no bank robber. Least ways not a successful one."

"You got that right, buddy. So who are you?"

"I am the Crimson Mask and I am here to ask you some questions. I already talked to your confederate, Barney Rouse, and he spilled everything he knew to me. Now I want to know all you know about this scheme. Will you cooperate and maybe get a softer deal from the judge, or do we have to do this the hard way," the masked man stated harshly.

"Oh, no, look, I'm no hero, and I'm no tough guy, and I certainly don't owe the fella that set this mess up anything at all. I'll spill. Just tell me what you want to know. I'm not stupid enough to go up against the Crimson Mask. I heard all about you."

"So then, start at the beginning and tell me about it," Clarke demanded.

Peach opened up and told his story to the masked man seated across from him and it was much like what Rouse had stated earlier. Peach received his instructions the same way, in the Park, he never saw the Mystery Man, and he had no idea who the man might be.

"What about when he handed you the plans, and when he took your money, did you see his hands?" Clarke asked carefully.

"Yeah, but only for a second," Peach replied casually.

"Did you notice anything about his hands?" Clarke continued just as casually. He didn't want to mention anything about the pinky ring and put any ideas into the man's head. He wanted to get real clues untainted by previous testimony or leading questions, but Peach seemed to be a far less observant fellow than Rouse had been.

"Nah, they was hands, that's all. I only saw them for a second. Didn't notice anything special about them at all."

"Well, then, what about the man's voice?" Clarke added.

"It was deep, like he was trying to disguise it."

Clarke nodded, "You ever hear that voice before?"

"Nah, never, it was nothing I ever heard before."

"Well, thank you, Mr. Peach," the Crimson Mask stated as he got up from his seat to leave the room.

"Hey! You'll talk to the cops for me? Talk to the judge, right? You promised. I spilled all I knew," Peach pleaded, looking for short time.

"You did and I will," then the Crimson Mask was gone.

Over in Brooklyn Sandra Gray pulled up her sleek roadster to Sammy Bolt's pawn shop on Gold Street and entered the dingy store.

All was quiet and Bolt was nowhere to be seen. Sandy took a careful look around and then drew the .38 out of her purse and held it out ready for action as she whispered, "Mr. Bolt? Mr. Bolt, are you here? It's me, Sandra Gray. Mr. Bolt?"

There was no answer to her pleas. Sandy walked farther into the store warily, passed multiple display cases of pawned items, she passed showcase after showcase of jewelry, guns, musical instruments, and other items of value, and then she saw him.

"Mr. Bolt!" Sandy screamed, holstering her gun as she rushed over to the prone form of the man on the floor behind the counter. She immediately felt for a pulse and found none, then she rolled him over and noticed the two bullet holes in the man's chest. He'd been shot in front, probably by someone he knew—or someone he never even suspected.

Sandy used the store phone to call Dave at the drug store, to relay the message to Bob Clarke. Then she called the cops. Afterwards she got into her roadster and got out of there and headed back into Manhattan and the drug store on East Avenue and Carmody Street.

Dave Small was running the counter back at the drug store when Bob Clarke walked in with Sandra Gray and Ted Warrick in tow.

"Dave, close it up, then come into the back room. We have much to discuss."

"Now you're talking, Boss!"

Behind the steel door of the secret back room Bob Clarke, Sandra Gray and Ted Warrick sat at a table as Dave Small entered.

"So what's the deal, Bob? Sandy called me with the news about Bolt," Ted Warrick asked.

"Yes, Sammy Bolt is dead. He was murdered, undoubtedly by the Mystery Man, who is no longer just a robber but a murderer as well now. A most dangerous man. Bolt must have guessed who the man is and that was his death warrant," Clarke told the former police commissioner.

"That's too bad," Dave said.

"I kinda liked the guy, though he was a weird old cuss," Sandy stated sadly. "He certainly didn't deserve that kind of end. He was trying to help us, Bob."

"I know."

"Well, what now?" Ted asked his friend.

"What did you learn from the men Inspector Blaine caught?" Dave asked Bob.

"Not much, this Mystery Man has set his plans very well. There may be another five or ten robberies planned for tonight at other Security National Bank branches. Or perhaps tomorrow. I've informed Blaine and he has men stationed at all the branches in the city. For now we play the waiting game. We'll see what happens tomorrow morning when the banks open their doors and if we find anyone in those vaults. Then we'll know if this so-called mastermind has been able to lure any more thieves into his scheme."

"I'm sure he has, Bob," Sandy said.

"Maybe," Clarke replied carefully, lighting up a cigarette and puffing away in deep thought. "You know, the more I think about this case, the more questions I have about it."

"Yeah, you and me both," Dave added grimly.

"Did you learn anything from the two men Inspector Blaine has in custody?" Ted Warrick asked.

"Nothing much, it was all done very neatly, controlled, neither thief ever saw the man they met, his voice was also obviously disguised, but one of the men, Rouse did notice something that might be helpful. He saw a coiled snake gold pinky ring on the mastermind's right hand."

Dave whistled, "That might prove helpful, Boss, but how do we find this guy?"

Clarke nodded, "Good question. The more I think about this case, the more it comes back to the design flaw that was noticed by the original thief, this mastermind dubbed by the papers as 'The Mystery Man.' He noticed the design flaw in the safety deposit boxes in the bank vaults. That has to be the key."

"You proposing that it was an inside job, Boss?" Dave asked, curious.

"Maybe," was all that Clarke answered, but he spoke softly, not entirely convinced of the theory yet. "I'm missing something here."

"What about the managers of the two branches that were hit? Either of them wear such a snake pinky ring?" Warrick asked hopefully, taking the ball and running with the inside job theory.

"No, and I spoke to both of them in person," Clarke stated firmly. "I would have noticed such an obvious piece of jewelry. No, it is not either of them, but it may be some manner of inside job, it almost has to be, but it was not those two men."

"What about another manager? From another branch?" Dave offered.

"What about someone who works in those branches, or at another one, a teller, clerk, maybe even a guard?" Warrick speculated.

"I have a feeling I need to aim a bit higher," Clarke said softly. "We have a few hours left of the day until the banks close. Here's what we'll do. Dave, I want you to go and question the manager and staff of the Lexington Avenue branch about anyone who wears a gold coiled snake pinky ring on their right hand. It may be some bank employee, but it may also be a customer. Keep that in mind. Sandy, you'll go to the 42nd Street branch and make the same inquiries there. Call in to Ted here with anything you find out and he'll relay the information to me."

"What about you, Boss?" Dave asked.

"The Crimson Mask is going to pay a visit to Mr. Simon Lowe, the owner and president of the Security National Bank system and see if he can come up with some answers," Clarke said sternly.

The trio left the drug store, stationing Ted Warrick there to coordinate any news. Dave Small was glad to finally be out of the store now and on the case, doing an actual investigation. He reached the Security National Bank on Lexington Avenue before it closed and began an intensive questioning of the manager and staff. It was not long before he found out what he needed to know and called in to Ted back at the store with his news.

Sandra Gray, likewise, drove to the bank branch on 42nd Street and had a good heart-to-heart talk with the manager there, as well as his staff. It was not long before she got a name for the man with the snake ring—a name that surprised her and made her suddenly fear for Bob when she was told exactly who the man was. Sandy immediately called her discovery in to Ted back at the store.

Ted Warrick took down the information that came in from both Dave and Sandy hours later. It was identical so he was sure it had to be good. He got the man's name and his whereabouts, but he was shocked and surprised once he realized the identity of the man with the snake ring. This was bad. Very dangerous. Ted knew he had to get in touch with Bob

Clarke right away with this information, but doing so was not an easy matter. Bob was now at Simon Lowe's secluded mansion on Long Island, and he knew it might be difficult, if not impossible, to get a phone message through to Bob without suspicion. Nevertheless, he had to try.

Ted Warrick placed his call to Bob Clarke at the home of the bank's president, Simon Lowe. He only hoped he could get through to Bob and warn him before it was too late.

The Lowe Mansion on Long Island was quite a lovely estate surrounded by tall trees and a running brook that Bob Clarke had heard boasted good fresh-water fishing almost year round. However, right now, he was only concerned with the people inside the house and what they might know about the bank robberies. As he approached the mansion he could hear the inside phone ringing, ringing wildly, almost frantically, then it suddenly stopped.

It was then that the Crimson Mask entered the house.

Simon Lowe was in his study alone, apparently catching up on some bank paperwork at his desk, when the door to the room suddenly burst open to reveal framed in the doorway the tall figure of a darkly dressed man with a red domino mask upon his face.

The old man startled, looked up with shock and shouted, "I know who you are! The Crimson Mask! What are you doing here? What do you want?"

"You know that I am assisting the city police by investigating these so-called Mystery Man robberies of your bank branches?" Clarke asked simply.

"Yes, I am aware of your involvement, two of my branch managers have reported the fact to me, as has Inspector Thomas Blaine of the city police," Lowe replied in growing concern as he looked at the fearful image that stood before him. "But what do you want here? I know nothing of any of this. Why are you here now?"

The Crimson Mask walked farther into the room, closer to the large ornate desk where Simon Lowe was seated. The masked man could see the nervous sweat upon the banker's face now. He was nervous, fearful. What did he know? Was it just the man's natural fear of a masked intruder? Or something else?

Many people in the city were not quite sure if the Crimson Mask was a criminal himself or a crime fighter—or both! Most people hardly knew how to react to him at all, especially the wealthy and powerful who often had mixed feelings and hidden motives for many of their actions. Clarke looked carefully at the man seated in front of him, his face, his form, and then focused closely at the various rings upon his fingers. There were quite a few. There was a gold wedding band on the left hand, a school ring there as well, and a small signet type ring on the pinky of the right hand. These were the only rings the man wore. Bob Clarke sighed deeply, it was a temporary defeat. There was no gold coiled snake pinky ring there at all, just as Clarke had been ready to assume. So now the game changed yet again.

"Mr. Lowe, I need your help in finding the man responsible for robbing your banks," Clarke said softly, in a more even tone now. "Will you help me?"

"Of course, I desire to see these robberies stopped as soon as possible, they are terrible for business, let me tell you," the banker responded in haste.

"Good. Then I have just one question for you. I believe you have a man working for you somewhere in your organization, a man who wears a gold coiled snake pinky ring on his right hand, do you not?"

Lowe looked up into the face of the masked man before him curiously, "Why, yes, I do. How did you know that?"

"Mr. Lowe, I need to know the name of that man and where I can find him," Clarke stated firmly.

The sudden sound of a revolver being cocked was unmistakable. The sound came from very close behind Clarke. He knew to stand frozen and not move. Meanwhile, Simon Lowe looked up and over, saw the man who had just entered the room but he did not notice the weapon he held and merely said, "Ah, there you are Jeremy. I have someone here who would like to speak to you."

"Really, Mr. Lowe," the voice of the newcomer answered harshly as the intruder moved closer to the masked man. The barrel of his revolver now pressed hard into to back of the Crimson Mask. The man named Jeremy was now right behind the Crimson Mask and carefully whispered into his ear, "Say one word or make one move and I will put a bullet into your back. Understand?"

Bob Clarke nodded gravely.

"Jeremy, this is the Crimson Mask," Lowe continued, oblivious of what was actually occurring as he continued to look down at the papers in front of him. It was obvious to Clarke that the old man was not actually aware of all that was going on right in front of him. Lowe continued, "He is investigating these robberies and would like to ask you some questions. Do you think you can help him?"

"Indeed, Mr. Lowe," Jeremy stated coldly. "I shall endeavor to do my best."

"Well that is just fine, Jeremy," Lowe said, now looking up at the Crimson Mask and indicating the newcomer, "This is my secretary and confidant, Jeremy Ambrose Mowbry, he has my full trust and I am sure he will be able to help you with any questions you may have," Lowe added with an imperious wave of his hand. The interview was over.

"And he wears a gold coiled snake pinky ring on his right hand?" Clarke stated, as Jeremy pushed the gun barrel harder into his spine.

"Be careful," Jeremy whispered into Clarke's ear. Then he stated coldly, "Yes, I do."

"Well, then why don't you both go into the Conservatory to discuss your business and leave me to finish up here on my own," Lowe said a bit tersely, impatient to get back to work and still obliviously unaware of what was actually taking place in front of him.

"Excellent idea, that's just what we shall do, Mr. Lowe. Sorry for the interruption, we shall endeavor to be as quiet as church mice," Jeremy replied, giving the revolver another push into Clarke's back, as he whispered menacingly, "You heard the old gent. Turn around and walk out of here, and if you try any funny stuff I won't hesitate to shoot you dead."

"All right," Clarke said, slowly turning and allowing himself to be led out of Simon Lowe's study, through the large oak doors, and then across the hallway and into the Conservatory.

When the two men were alone Jeremy closed the Conservatory door behind him, and then waved his gun to motion the Crimson Mask further into the room. The two men were standing barely five feet apart with Jeremy's revolver aimed solidly at the heart of the Crimson Mask.

"So you found out all about my neat trick?" Jeremy asked.

"You were masterful in discovering the design flaw in the vault. How did you find it?" Clarke asked the man with genuine admiration.

"Thank you. Coming from you, that is indeed a compliment. I noticed the plans on Mr. Lowe's desk one day when I began working for him a few months ago. I saw right away the possibilities. It was too good to resist." Jeremy stated with evident pride. "I did the first two robberies myself, just to see what it was like, but I am not a bank robber by nature, so I set up a plan to franchise the robberies and make myself some money."

"Well, it was nothing short of brilliant," the Crimson Mask stated.

Jeremy smiled broadly, "Your compliments are gratifying. You are making it harder for me to do what I know I must do."

"And what's that?" Bob Clarke asked, knowing all too well that Jeremy had slated him for immediate execution, but wanting to get the man to admit it in his own words.

"You have botched up all my plans and caused me considerable difficulties that I am not sure I can set right," Jeremy added in a grim dark tone.

"Well, you can still turn yourself in to me now, and I will see to it that you receive a fair trial," Clarke told the man.

"Hah! Crimson Mask, you forget that I am the one holding the gun! I am the talk of the town, the Mystery Man, and I am afraid that this city is not big enough for the two of us."

"That is true," Clarke stated, adding, "but you have no chance of escape, your identity is known. It is all over for you."

"Perhaps, but Mr. Lowe is…forgetful in his old age. You are the only witness that I can see, and a dead witness is hardly any kind of witness at all."

"So you plan to murder me?" Clarke asked. "Like you murdered Sammy Bolt?"

"Of course," Jeremy said simply. "Mr. Bolt followed one of my men and saw me. He did not know who I was but he could not remain alive with that knowledge."

The Crimson Mask smiled; he had noticed that Jeremy had not immediately fired his revolver to end his life. The man was holding back for some reason. Clarke was sure that it was not for fear of adding one more murder to his list. Bob Clarke thought he saw another answer to that question and waited for what was to come.

Jeremy finally said, "But first, before I kill you, there is something that has been preying upon my mind. I need to know who the man is behind that red domino mask. I want to be the man who reveals the identity of the Crimson Mask!"

"I wouldn't do that if I were you," Bob Clarke growled in dire warning.

"You are forgetting I have the gun here. Why, I'll pull that red mask right off your face if I want. In fact, I think I'll do it right now, right here, and there's not a damn thing you can do to stop me," Jeremy boasted loudly, waving his pistol menacingly.

"I think not," Clarke growled.

"Well, I think I shall do it!"

"Then go ahead, give it a try," Clarke offered in menacing warning.

Jeremy looked at the tall, red-masked figure with a sudden hint of fear, then smiled that fear away with renewed confidence, after all it was he who held the gun, not his helpless victim.

Jeremy pointed the gun at Clarke's head, the same spot where his police sergeant father had been shot and killed so many years before. Clarke's face instantly turned red with anger, a fire suddenly burned throughout his entire body, searing his mind with blind rage he could barely hold in check.

Jeremy continued, "I am the Mystery Man and now I am going to unmask the Crimson Mask and discover your true identity. I will do this before I kill you, while you are still alive, so I can witness your utter defeat and humiliation. Then I am going to empty this revolver into your head, one slug at a time, until your face truly turns into a crimson mask! How fitting is that? How do you like that?"

Bob Clarke allowed a dire grimace that somehow totally unnerved Jeremy Ambrose Mowbry even as he tightly held his weapon pointed at the masked man.

"Then you do it! Remove it now!" Jeremy demanded, "Or I will rip that mask off your face myself!"

Clarke carefully reached up with his left hand and slowly removed the red domino mask from his face to reveal his true identity.

Both men were silent for a long moment, looking intently at each other, then...

"Why...? I know you!" Jeremy blurted in sudden shock and recognition.

"You wanted to know, so now you know," Clarke said, suddenly withdrawing the hidden .38 from behind his back and pulling the trigger that put one well-placed slug squarely into the center of Jeremy's forehead. The attack had been so quick, so immediate, Jeremy never anticipated it. He had not even been able to return one shot.

Jeremy Ambrose Mowbry fell to the floor of the Conservatory with a stark look of total surprise upon his face, his body stone dead.

Bob Clarke replaced his mask and returned the .38 to the secreted holster behind his back. Then he calmly walked out of the room and across the hall into the study to inform Mr. Lowe that the robberies of his banks had been solved and that he would have no further problems in that area.

"Well ... Why, thank you, Crimson Mask," Lowe replied, happily elated now by the good news. He did not deign to get up from his desk to thank the man physically, to shake his hand, or even to ask any further questions. Instead he looked at the masked man and said nervously, "I don't know if it is true what people say about you. You know they say some pretty bad things …"

"They're all true, I'm afraid, Mr. Lowe," the Crimson Mask stated grimly without any humor at all.

Lowe took it all quite differently than intended. He merely laughed with a mild cackle, "Of course. So it is all settled then?"

"Yes," Clarke stated, "but you will need to hire a new confidential secretary. I regret to inform you that as of this moment Mr. Jeremy Ambrose Mowbry is no longer in your employ. You should also place a call to the local police."

"Really?"

"Yes, really," Clarke admitted softly. "Next time you hire a confidential secretary you should check his past."

The phone on Lowe's desk suddenly rang. Distracted and annoyed by the interruption he picked it up shouting, "Why so many calls tonight! Confounded salesmen! Yes, what is it?" he barked, then he allowed himself to listen for a moment and with obvious surprise handed the receiver to the Crimson Mask.

"It's for you," Lowe added in astonishment.

"Yes?" Clarke answered. It was Ted Warrick at the other end of the line back at the drug store.

"Bob, that you? Thank God! I've been trying to get in touch with you all night! Must have called a dozen times …"

"Yes, Ted?"

"I got frantic when Dave and Sandy said they found out who the man with the gold snake ring is."

"Jeremy Ambrose Mowbry," Clarke stated firmly. "I know, Ted, it's all taken care of now."

"You all right? Sandy's worried sick, we all are."

Bob Clarke allowed a soft laugh, "I'm fine, Ted. Tell Sandy I'm fine, and Ted…tell her I love her…and that I …"

"I will, Bob," Ted answered quickly.

Clarke handed the receiver back to Mr. Lowe who quickly hung it up, staring at the masked man before him with a mixture of awe and simple confusion.

"Good evening, Mr. Lowe," then as silently as he had appeared, the Crimson Mask was gone for good.

The End

BEHIND THE CRIMSON MASK

He was an intense character, a relentless crime fighter and one of the coolest of pulp heroes, in my opinion—even though he did not have his own magazine like better known masked pulp heroes. I hope you feel the same way I do about this masked avenger after you read my story in this anthology, "The Mystery Man". Through the fine efforts of the Airshp27 team, the Crimson Mask does the pulps one better: he never had his own magazine, but now for the first time ever, he has his own book of stories!

My own story in this book required quite a bit of research which was fun to do. I enjoyed reading the original stories written by Frank Johnson—actually legendary pro pulp scribe Norman Daniels. Daniels wrote fifteen Crimson Mask stories between 1940 and 1944, but they are difficult to locate today in the original pulp magazines published over sixty years ago. Some were reprinted in the 1970s by Bob Weinberg and other publishers, and many of these I am happy to have in my book collection. So I read them, and I enjoyed them very much. However, I knew it would be a real challenge to write my new Crimson Mask tale, but it was a joy all the same.

In writing my story I made every effort to keep it true to the flavor of the original Daniels tales. I wanted the main character, Doc Clarke, and his team of compatriots, to ring true to their pulp origins. Once I had the feel of the characters down, I set about to involve them in a crime tale that has some unique aspects to it—that of a robbery spree being conducted as a franchise crime operation. I think that's an idea that has not been done that often, if ever. It proved to be a challenge for myself as a writer, as well as the Crimson Mask himself. I hope you like the results and if you do, demand to see more stories of the crime fighter who wears the red velvet domino mask.

GARY LOVISI is a Mystery Writers of America Edgar Award nominee and Western Writers of America Spur Award winner for his writing and editing. His latest books, all out now, include *Sherlock Holmes: The Baron's Revenge* (Airship27 Productions, tpb and e-book); *Mars Needs Books!* (Wildside Press, tpb), a dytopian science fiction novel about bookmen on Mars; and the edited anthology, *Battling Boxing Stories* (Wildside Press, tpb). Lovisi is the founder of Gryphon Books, editor of *Paperback Parade* and *Hardboiled* magazines, and is the sponsor of an annual book collectors show in New York City, now in its 25th year. To find out more about him, his work, or Gryphon Books, visit his web site at: www.gryphonbooks.com.

The Blood of the Mob
By C. William Russette

Theodore Warrick, retired police commissioner, opened the side door without bothering to check through the window who it was. It was that unique doorbell ring. Steady eyes stared back, serious but not without warmth. The man standing on the back stoop was a stranger but at the same time not completely unfamiliar. The stranger wore a black hat and a suit to match. He bore a well trimmed moustache and his jowls puffed out from being slightly overweight.

Warrick smiled at his long time friend Bob Clarke, alias the Crimson Mask.

"You could pass me on the subway and I'd never have known it was you," Warrick said and stepped back to let Clarke in.

"Then my disguise has done its job," Clarke said.

It was midnight but both were used to keeping the hours of criminals. Warrick closed the door and followed Clarke into the living room.

"What have you got?" Clarke said.

"Detective Norton came by today. He said the police have a case with the stink of weird to it. He asked me to contact the Crimson Mask as soon as I could."

"Go on."

"Two murders, seven months apart, similar causes of death. Gaetano Reina was found hanging by the neck in his basement seven months ago. Initially they thought it was a suicide. A few nights ago Joseph 'Fat Joe' Pinzolo was found strangled in an office building that was still under construction."

"You said *initially* they thought it was a suicide?"

"There was a symbol on the victim's chest over the breastbone."

"Was it a tattoo?"

"No, it was carved into his skin."

"Was it messy? Around the mark?"

"Coroner thought it was done after he hung himself."

"So it was done *to* him. Any suspects?"

"The police didn't find any leads. Cops don't chase after murdered mob guys too hard."

"I suspect Fat Joe was a member of the mob as well."

"He had the same symbol cut into his chest."

"Did Norton bring a photograph of the symbol?"

Warrick picked up a manila folder from the coffee table and handed it to Clarke. Inside were two photographs and some handwritten notes. They were torso shots of the victims. Someone had written the names in the top right corner of each in red marker. Clarke examined the necks of both corpses. Ligature marks on Reina's neck were consistent with hanging by some sort of rope. The bruised skin of Pinzola's neck implied strangulation by hand. Someone with big hands and strong arms killed Fat Joe. A body thrashes violently when being strangled. You have to have strength, determination and privacy. That explained the empty office building where Pinzola was found.

Clarke pulled a small magnifying glass out of his breast pocket. He held it over the breastbone of first the Reina photograph then Pinzola's. Something very sharp, in a steady hand made the delicate cuts that formed the symbols. They were the same design: a diamond shape standing on an upside down 'V'. The crime scenes of both bodies were written on the backs of the photos.

"What do you think?" Warrick finally asked.

"I'm not familiar with this symbol but I will be. As far as the victims go it appears like we have two Italian mob guys that got into something bigger than they are. I won't know more until I start my investigation."

"Detective Norton thought it would be better if he brought it to you before letting the Bureau of Investigation know. They always step on toes when they barge into town."

"You can let Detective Norton know that the Crimson Mask will take the case," Clarke said.

Crime scenes deteriorate quickly. The Crimson Mask headed to the office building where Pinzola was found. The Reina scene was surely trampled and examined to death by now.

The Mask had changed his disguise, this time to a slim, slouched, poorly dressed man, before driving to the office building on the edge of the Bronx. He had memorized the addresses in the folder. The Mask parked a few blocks away and casually walked to the construction site.

The construction firm erecting the building was named D'Arco Limited. There weren't many new companies sprouting up due to the country's economic status. The Mask knew D'Arco was mob connected. It would be easy to slip in, whack someone and get out if you could control the site's comings and goings.

But why would you use a site that you knew might be tied to you? The Mask hopped the chain link fence. The three story structure had yet to receive walls or a roof. Fortunately there were no windows installed. The Mask eased through the closest window and turned on his flashlight.

They hadn't wanted the murder to be seen from the street. It could have attracted attention too soon if the murder was observed only half finished. It would have been done deeper inside, he guessed.

He squatted down and shone the flashlight on the wooden floor. A layer of dust covered everything. The Mask checked the walls and the ceiling. Whereever the drywall met, the seams were spackled and sanded, explaining some of the dust. The Mask walked to the hall and noted the variety of footprints moving to the right, outside, and to the left, deeper into the building.

The Crimson Mask turned left down the hall.

He didn't have far to go. He had entered through what might be an office. The adjoining hallway where he found the footprints was likely to be the main thoroughfare between a mirror image of the area he had just passed through. There were some closets and a restroom and then what had to be a conference room. The Mask scanned the floor. It was awash in footprints. He entered the room and walked the perimeter, keeping as close to the wall as possible. There were fewer prints there and it allowed him to reach the exits. There were very few footprints by any of the room's three exits. That meant the majority of the action had taken place in this room.

The Crimson Mask began to study the footprints in the room and sort through them to discern between the police, murderer and the victim. Carefully the Mask began to scour the days-old crime scene.

He found out everything he could in a few hours' time. What he discovered puzzled him. He stored the information away as there was still more to gather before a conclusion or action could be made. The Mask left the building and returned to his Chevrolet.

The Crimson Mask needed more information and he knew exactly where to get it.

It was a short drive to the Palatial Hotel in Midtown Manhattan. When he drove the streets, Clarke never wore the velvet domino mask. The less the enemy could learn about you, like your car make, the better off you and those you cared about were.

Emil Gizzo was a snitch. Warrick had turned the Mask on to him years before. The cops used him on occasion but mostly they wanted to keep him in play and alive. As the doorman to the speakeasy in the basement of the Palatial, Gizzo saw and heard a lot of things; things the Mask was interested in knowing.

Bob Clarke didn't have to wait long before Gizzo came out to the parking lot for a cigarette. If he wasn't prone to long breaks he would be missed. Clarke knew he had to act fast. Out of a secret pocket in his black coat the Crimson Mask retrieved his red velvet mask.

Gizzo's attentiveness was as short as his stature. He stood smoking a few feet from the building's brick wall. The Mask had him by the lapels and off his feet before he had time to squeak out a puff of smoke.

"Hey! I told you coppers I ain't workin' for you no—"

"Quiet, Gizzo."

"The Crimson—"

The Mask pressed his hand over Gizzo's mouth.

"I said quiet. You're going to answer some questions for me and quick."

"I don't know nothing! I just open the door and let rich people come in and get a little cabbage for doin' a good job, right?"

Gizzo found himself lifted higher off the ground and slammed against the wall of the Palatial.

"One more time! I *want* to know who killed Fat Joe Pinzola!"

"Easy! No need to get rough. I don't know no Pinzola anyway."

"What about Gaetano Reina?"

Gizzo hesitated for just a second, his eyes darted left and right.

"Nope, sorry, Mask. Never heard of him neither."

The Mask lowered Gizzo to the ground.

"I wonder if you're telling the truth, Gizzo." The Mask straightened Gizzo's lapels.

"'Course I am."

"Well, maybe I'll just ask around inside. Maybe someone in there will be familiar with Reina and Pinzola. Maybe they can tell me why after years of devoted service to both me and the police department, you are suddenly so uninformed. I'll be right back." The Mask started down the steps to the basement speakeasy.

"What? C'mon, like yer gonna go in there with them types. Everybody knows about you and wants you dead! They'd blast you in a second."

"Are you willing to bet I can't get their attention with a tale about *you* before that happens? Even if they do get me, imagine what they'll do to you?"

"Reina was head of a family! Okay?"

"It's a start." The Mask remained on the cement stairs.

"He ran a family in the Bronx. I think maybe I heard that Pinzola guy was part of the crew too… maybe. It's all rumor though. I won't swear to nothing."

The Crimson Mask returned to Gizzo.

"Go on."

"What go on? That's all I got."

The Crimson Mask's gloved hand lashed out. He gripped Gizzo's upper lip between his index and middle knuckles.

Gizzo voiced a twisted and brief howl. "The Reina gang runs the ice racket! He was the go-to guy to get your ice delivered all over the city for like ten years! I heard he was running hooch too. He was on his way to being even bigger 'til he got killed!" Gizzo said.

"So who killed him, Gizzo?"

"How the hell do I know?"

The Mask tightened his fist and Gizzo squealed.

"Ask Masseria! I heard they was tight. Now lemme go already!"

The Crimson Mask did, stepped back and melted into the shadows.

"I may return, Gizzo. If I do you had better be more accommodating."

"Yeah, right… whatever." Gizzo lit another cigarette and massaged his face.

The American Ice Company warehouse was the biggest of the five that the Mask visited that night. It was still just one story but seemed to be spread out over more square footage. Since the mass production of the electric refrigerator the ice industry had been rapidly shrinking. Three of the city's ice warehouses were out of business or soon would be according to the signing outside. One, the National Ice Company, was closed for the night but would be open soon to make deliveries. The American Ice company was not only the most secured behind its chain link fence but it was also the best known. Curiously it was the only one open at this late hour.

The Crimson Mask parked his car a few blocks away. He casually walked to the warehouse; he scaled the fence and landed on the other side without a sound. His crepe-soled shoes concealed the sound of his steps. He ran through the parking lot seeking shadows in the poorly lit area. Only one section of the warehouse had windows illuminated from within.

Maybe there were industrious workers inside that didn't mind or couldn't afford not to work third shift. Maybe it was the cleaning crew. Maybe it was an accountant working late crossing his Ts and dotting his Is. The Mask knew it was none of those things. All the cars in the section closest to the building—three of them-—were expensive Packards.

There could be anywhere from three to twenty men in there, the Crimson Mask thought. He knew he would have to play it smart, if he wanted to make it out of this without getting ventilated. There was also the point of getting the information he needed if he was going to make any progress on this case.

The parking lot entrance wasn't locked. These guys were confident that they could handle anyone dumb enough to step into their property. How many have guns? Best to assume they all do. Never underestimate your enemy. It was the quickest way to get dead.

Dr. Bob Clarke retrieved his crimson mask from his suit's secret pocket and put it on.

The Crimson Mask eased the metal door shut and waited. Hearing nothing he touched his right hand to the wall on the same side and stepped forward in silence. There were no sounds when he reached the end of the drywall. Directly above him was a large circular mirror atop a sign warning about forklift safety. Straight ahead and to the left were great racks stacked two levels high. Around the corner to his right, was a man in a cheap suit and hat with both arms folded over his chest. He stood in front of another metal door that likely led to the stairs.

It was a straight run at the man. If he was armed, and he likely was, he would cut down the Mask easily before he took a half-dozen steps. Running straight to the racks and trying to go around would be a gamble, too. There might be a way around the vast, dark building to come up behind the man but one chance look over his shoulder and there would be gunfire. The Crimson Mask knew he couldn't just shoot him, as the noise would bring more men and he could be cornered easily in these unfamiliar surroundings.

It had to be silent. The Crimson Mask looked up and smiled. He walked over to the doors he just entered through and kicked one open then slammed it shut; then he hid himself.

The guard stepped softly though still loud enough for the Crimson Mask to hear, and peaked around the corner at the doors. He saw nothing and stepped all the way around but with care. The man quick-stepped towards the entrance with his handgun drawn. He looked eager to use it.

The Crimson Mask had not made a sound since slamming the door, still this guard was wary. He had good instincts and stayed close to the wall while looking around. He looked out the small rectangular window in the door to the parking lot.

Nothing. Maybe a gust of wind had opened the unlocked door? The man sighed and holstered his gun. Calmly he started back to his post. The Crimson Mask leaped down off the low roof of the drywall office and onto his back. The guard tried to regain his senses but the Crimson Mask landed a powerful roundhouse that bounced the thug's head off the cement floor. The thug fell unconscious.

The Crimson Mask grabbed the sleeping man under his arms and dragged him into the small office. He closed the door and raced for the stairwell. The old door opened noisily. He eased it shut and waited in the darkness.

No one called out, no one came to investigate the sound. He was alone in the stairwell and jogged up the stairs to the second floor.

"I want some fresh air," a voice said from above. "That okay with you? What are ya, my mother? I'll be back in five."

The second floor door opened just as the Mask made the landing. He stepped behind the door. A man in a cheap suit appeared putting his hat on and saw nothing. Before he could step down the stairs, the Crimson Mask took him by the collar and swung him into the cinderblock wall. The Mask threw a jab hitting the gangster on the chin and his head bounded off the wall again. The thug collapsed like a sack of wet cement. The Mask caught his hat as he fell, then eased him out of his coat and removed his mask.

The impromptu disguise wouldn't hold up under close inspection but maybe it would get him a little closer to the man running the ice operation. The thug was armed only with a blackjack. The Mask took it.

The second floor stairwell opened up to several offices. The wooden floor was worn but felt sturdy enough. The hallway branched off to the right where the floor continued and straight ahead where it was carpeted. Most likely the managers' offices were along the latter aisle. It was a good bet the maintenance crews were expected to use the wooden floor to spare the carpet.

The Crimson Mask heard a commotion in the first office down the carpeted hall and dashed to the right. He was one man, with six bullets available before reloading. If they were armed with more than a sap or blackjack his odds of escaping alive went far down.

There had to be another entrance to the offices that didn't have a gaggle of goofs hooting and hollering over a card game. The Mask turned left at the end of the hallway where it was darkest. At the far end of the corridor light spilled out of an entryway to the offices.

Bingo.

Maybe the head guy had his office away from the rattling of his men? A paranoid leader would have a stoolie planted among his crew, whereas a smart boss desiring trust and loyalty would remain amongst his men to built good faith and camaraderie. A man who worked through fear would want to keep his distance. The Mask considered every angle.

The door was closed at the first office but the Mask could see through the windows on either side of it. There was a light inside. The Mask stepped onto the well trodden carpet. He could still hear the yelling down the hall. He listened at the door, heard nothing, then barged in.

"What the hell are you—" said the grey haired man behind the cheap desk.

The Crimson Mask crashed a blackjack across his mouth. The man fell back into his chair, covered his mouth with one hand and reached for his desk drawer with the other. The Mask brought the blackjack down on his wrist eliciting another grunt of pain. The Mask took a 1911 automatic pistol from the drawer and pocketed it.

The Crimson Mask dashed to the door and locked it.

"Be smart and that's the end of the violence between us." The Mask locked the office door. "Forget how to think and it goes downhill from here."

"I know you. You're that Crimson Mask guy."

"Guilty as charged. What's your name?"

"George." He sucked on his teeth.

"Do you have a last name, George?"

"Alfani if you gotta know. Yer gonna be dead soon anyway so who cares?"

"I know this ice operation was part of the Reina gang. I also know that you are a part of that gang. I'm here for what I don't know. Like why Gaetano Reina was whacked. Was it by a rival gang? Internal strife? Tell me a story, George."

"Gaetano who? I dunno what yer talkin' about, mister masked man. I am running a legit business here. I provide a product people need and I am paid for it. You're the one broke in here and assaulted me."

"Are you going to tell me that you've never heard of Fat Joe Pinzola either? They found him dead this week. Someone is killing gangsters, Alfani, and the trail leads here."

"Some prick gets strangled and I should care why?"

The Crimson Mask charged forward shoving the desk hard, pinning Alfani to the wall. He wheezed out a cough but couldn't get leverage with his arms to free himself.

"Who said anything about getting strangled, Alfani? Spill it!"

"Okay! Christ on a crutch, back off so's I can breathe! I dunno who whacked Reina. No one does. I *just* heard that Fat Joe was strangled. I don't know nothin' about it."

The Crimson Mask applied pressure to his side of the desk. "You're going to have to do better than that if you want that big breath of air."

"I dunno why Reina was killed. It's the truth! Fat Joe was brought in after he was gone!"

"What do you mean *brought in*?"

"He wasn't one of us. He was one of Masseria's people."

That's the second time Masseria's name was dropped tonight.

The Crimson Mask had heard of Giuseppe "Joe the Boss" Masseria, though not often. He had been a name in the New York mob scene for many years. It was the mob that helped create the Crimson Mask in the first place. Had the mob not gunned down Bob Clarke's father, a police officer, when he was a boy there might not have been any reason for him to train himself in the ways of a law officer and fight crime not in the name of vengeance but for justice.

"Why would Masseria replace the leader of the Reina gang? That makes no sense."

"Him and Reina were working together like partners or something."

"On what?"

"How hell do I know? I work the ice racket."

"George, you okay in there?" someone asked on the other side of the door.

The Crimson Mask looked at the floor beneath where the desk had been only moments ago. There was a small paddle like one you might find under a sewing machine. The cord ran into the floor.

Alfani was smiling.

"Hey, look at that? Smart guy noticed. You really think I would just give over information if I thought you were gonna get out of here alive, stupido?"

"Why's the door locked, George?" the other side of the door asked.

"Who's running the Reina gang now?" the Crimson Mask asked.

"Screw you f—"

The Crimson Mask gripped Alfani's windpipe. Alfani choked and clawed at his attacker. Crimson Mask caught two fingers and bent them backwards. Alfani squirmed and tried to cough.

"I can come back every night for the rest of your life and do this, Alfani. Who is running the gang now?"

"I'm gonna kick in the door, George," the voice outside announced.

Alfani's face was beet-red. Sweat had broken out on his forehead. Alfani nodded.

Crimson Mask released his throat.

"Gagliano-Gagliano! I take orders from Tommy Gagliano."

It sounded familiar.

The door swung inside and slammed against the wall. The Crimson Mask was already closing in. Before the first goon could raise his gun, the Crimson Mask smashed the butt of his revolver into his face crushing his nose. The goon made a choking sound and reached for his face. The Crimson Mask shoved him back out into the hallway and into three more of his pals. All three fell over each other.

Two more were on the far side of the pile of thugs. The Crimson Mask didn't see any guns drawn and charged to the left. *No need to fight everyone if you didn't have to. Especially when I'm outnumbered.*

"He's headin' for the stairs!" someone shouted.

Drywall exploded with bullets behind him as the Crimson Mask disappeared around the corner. One or both of the pair were firing after him. The Mask wasn't about to stick around and see how good a shot either one of them were.

It was a straight run back to the stairs. Twenty feet from the stairway a goon as big as a football player swung a Thompson submachine-gun around the corner, right in front of where the Mask was heading. The Mask pivoted around then froze. One of the tangled goons from outside the office was aiming an automatic at him.

"You're dead!" the hood screamed.

The Crimson Mask dropped as flat as he could while the tommy-gun tried to home in on him. Both shooters started unloading their guns from opposite ends of the hallway into each other before they could stop

"The Crimson Mask was already closing in."

themselves. Both were down but only one was groaning. With any luck the fools down the hall were thinking it was the Mask that had the machinegun and would stay put. It might buy him the time he needed to escape before another shooter appeared.

The barrel of a second chopper poked around the corner. The crook squatted and checked on his dead companion. The Mask dropped to one knee while aiming his .38 pistol. The new gunner had just started to raise his weapon when he caught two rounds in the chest. The Crimson Mask was up and running before the man hit the floor.

There was nothing to be gained by sticking around. He had a name: Tommy Gagliano. He faintly recalled the name but he needed to jog his memory and he knew just the place for it.

The Crimson Mask passed the now squirming guard at the dual metal doors that was his exit. He could hear more troops charging out from the stairwell and getting closer.

There was a broom leaning against the rack opposite the drywall office. The Crimson Mask grabbed it without stopping. Once outside he broke the broomstick in two then drove both shafts through the door handles.

You're going to have to find another exit to catch me, boys.

"I can't believe you're still burning the midnight oil," the Crimson Mask said.

"Look who's talking. Yours aren't the only cases I still work, you know," Warrick said and closed the door behind him. "Coffee?"

"Sure. I'm here for a few answers." The Crimson Mask removed his hat and mask.

Warrick poured. "I guessed as much."

"What can you tell me about Tommy Gagliano?"

"Another member of the Reina gang wrapped up in this?"

Doc Clarke told Warrick what had happened.

"Well, far as I knew Gagliano was Reina's underboss, the gang's number two stooge. He has been for years. We never made any headway on nabbing him."

Warrick passed Clarke a steaming cup of coffee.

"He was never busted for anything and he had a head for business. He always looked like he had more dough than he should be making. Always had a driver, nice suits, never heard he was broke. We never caught him rolling a delivery truck or anything like that. Not even when he was coming up. I know he runs a speakeasy under the Diamonds club," Warrick informed.

Clarke sipped from his mug. "What doesn't fit is why Fat Joe jumped ahead of him, from another gang, when Reina died. Got anything on him?"

"Nothing that might help. I thought he was with Masseria."

"Joe Masseria. How does he fit into this?"

"Not sure. I know there was some kind of bad blood between Masseria and Maranzano. There is some kind of a turf war going on. I can look into it tomorrow once my guys wake up."

"Do that. I better get some shut-eye as well. Tomorrow night I'm going to have a chat with our friend, Tommy Gagliano."

Dr. Bob Clarke rose from bed after only a few hours sleep. Having trained for scenarios like this, Clarke's endurance had no problem compensating for little rest. He put on a pot of coffee, exercised for an hour, then showered and drank coffee with a poached egg. While finishing his second cup he went over the events of last night and what lay ahead of him.

At nine, Dr. Bob Clarke, druggist and pharmacist, entered his first floor drug store from the internal stairs. He took in the expanse of his one room bastion against the common ailments of man. All three counters were orderly and dust-free. Stock on the shelves was pushed to the front with labels facing forward. The free candy jars for the children were even topped off.

Dave Small's head appeared over the counter behind the candy jars.

"I thought I heard you, Bob. Good morning. Just checking on some of the stock; order goes in today, you know."

"Yes, I know."

"Anything interesting going on that you'd care to share with your old pal Dave?"

"It was a long and interesting night to be sure, my friend."

Clarke gave Dave an abbreviated version of the past night's events.

"I can handle the store if you need to rest, Bob."

"No, no. Warrick has given me a lot of information about these murders. It just takes time to follow up on them. Did I miss anything here yesterday?"

"Well Sandra called for you twice. Guess she was wondering if you two were still on for tonight at the Sea-Song restaurant?"

"Seven o'clock, if I recall. I'll give her a call later to be sure." Clarke walked the interior of the counter, checking stores.

"Why all this effort over some gangsters killing one another? Aren't we better off without them?" Dave asked.

"Even murderers deserve their day in court. What worries me most about this are the innocents that might get caught in the middle of some petty gang war." Clarke checked the secret red light beneath the counter. It flashed on and off.

The Crimson Mask was needed.

"Are we open, Dave?" Clarke asked while setting money into the cash register.

"It's after nine isn't it? Of course we are." Dave tilted his head.

"Did you unlock the door?"

"Yes?"

"Then why does the sign say closed?"

"Crud." Dave walked over to the door.

"I'll be back after my shift at the hospital."

Clarke closed the door that separated the show floor of the drug store from the supply room and laboratory. He locked the door and called Warrick.

"What's happened?"

"There's been another murder."

"Someone isn't messing around. Do we have a name?"

"Yes, it's George Alfani."

The line went silent on both ends.

Clarke did not want to go to work at City Hospital. He had no choice; appearances had to be maintained. For the sake of his friends, the Crimson Mask and Dr. Bob Clarke had to remain unconnected. It would look odd if every time some strange murder shook the city the Crimson Mask became more active and Dr. Clarke called in sick for a week.

The shift at the hospital wasn't completely unbearable. Besides being able to help those in need, Clarke took his lunch at the New York Public Library on 5th Avenue. It was close to the hospital and one of the most prominent research libraries in North America. If an answer was to be found, he felt it would be there.

Clarke was not mistaken. Not wanting to draw attention or give anyone cause to remember him, Clarke searched without staff help. He went to the file catalogue and tried ancient symbols, runes, and dead languages. Using such a large net he felt would surely catch something. Thanks to his medical training and rudimentary familiarity with Latin he ruled out that dead language immediately and cut the stack considerably. By the time he browsed the subject of runes he knew he was getting close.

The oldest form of the runic alphabet used by the Germanic tribes was called Elder Futhark. It dated as far back as the second century and a number of other runic alphabets were based off of it. The runes were inscribed on everything from artifacts to jewelry. There was no mention of corpses getting such a thing carved into them. He found the diamond shaped rune with the stick legs or stand or whatever it was on the bottom of the diamond in a number of runic alphabets.

Othala. It meant either homeland or ancestral lot or some kind of inheritance. Material holdings? Maybe. It governs power and knowledge from past generations or the acquisition of wealth. It is about the ascension to the rank of king from among the common man. Rising from your station in life to a much better place basically, Clarke thought. Inheritance can mean a lot of things. There's legal inheritance and rigging the vote as they say. Is that what the killer or killers was doing? Reina was taken out, the head or king of his family. Fat Joe was placed in his position and then seven months later he was taken out, too. Someone disapproved of the leadership in the Reina gang. Why? Who was supposed to be top dog?

Why was Alfani killed? Had he been tattooed as well?

Clarke's eyes floated over the open books in front of him. They kept coming back to the rune othala. Another word often appeared with it. Odin. It was a rune associated with someone named Odin. The name seemed familiar but digging deeper into his mind produced nothing. It took less than ten minutes to find a book that would reference the name.

Odin was a god; more so, he was a king of gods. Like Zeus in Greek mythology. Odin also had many children, like Zeus. One was called Thor. He sounded familiar but Clarke couldn't recall from where. Clarke was running out of time so he started skimming. Odin was a god of war, victory and death. Clarke wondered how many pantheons were ruled by death gods. The world was a strange place.

Stranger still was the manner in which the worshippers of Odin made sacrifices to their god. In Sweden, many males, including slaves, were hung from trees in offer to Odin.

They strangled to death.

"Tough day at the office, Bob?" Sandra asked. Her eyes were wide, her make-up perfect, her sarcasm unmistakable.

Bob Clarke tipped his hat back on his head with his index finger and wore a sincere face.

"We usually start the banter after I'm through the door, Sandy."

"Guess I got lost in the enthusiasm for the night ahead. Please come in." Sandy smiled, her eyes twinkled and she stepped back clearing the way for him to enter the apartment.

Clarke removed his hat as he crossed into the foyer and placed it on the coat rack. Her place wasn't big but it was perfect for a single woman with greater interests than those marital. *But then what choice did she have,* Clarke mused. She was stuck on Bob Clarke in the best way but the Crimson Mask had chained the church doors.

It was a crime laden city and needed his unique skills. There was no end in sight but Sandy was stubborn. She had agreed to wait for the day when there was no more need for the red-masked mystery man. She was an amazing woman and he knew he was damn fortunate to have her. He truly looked forward to the day when he could keep her at his side every night. Not just when injustice took a night off.

"Penny for your thoughts, Doc?" She shut the door and waited to take his coat.

He didn't take it off.

"I could never charge you for my thoughts, Sandy. No higher than a half penny for sure." Clarke smiled.

Sandy turned back to Clarke with mock anger on her face. She let Clarke take her in his arms and he kissed her. The passion threatened to boil over like magma in a trembling volcano. Using every ounce of his resolve Clarke broke free.

"Ready for a drink?" She stepped away from him, flushed, but controlling herself masterfully. She walked away to the wet bar and reached for the single malt Scotch.

"I'm afraid I can't."

"Tonight is off as well?"

"Tonight is postponed if you'll accept a rain check."

"I guess it depends on the date of the rain check, Doctor Clarke."

No mock anger now. No expression period.

"I will be back promptly after I take care of some very pressing business. You can set your watch by it."

"Oh, I intend to, mister. Would this be nocturnal work of a dangerous nature?"

Sandy stepped close to Clarke. Her grey eyes bored into his and he welcomed the heat.

"It could be for any other man."

"I can help you know. I *have* skills."

"You certainly do and normally I would call on them, but I would be worried about your safety. This case is different somehow."

"Is the Alfani murder tied into this?"

"It's already hit the rags?"

"Yes. I'm hearing rumors that he was connected to the mob. Is that true, Bob?"

"I'm not going to tell you anything for the same reason I won't let you help me."

"You think it will keep me safe. Fine. You better go then."

"You can get sore if it makes you feel better, Sandy, but I will not have you getting hurt helping me."

"What if *you* get hurt? Aren't you a man, same as those creeps?"

"I won't get hurt because I'll know you're safe and my mind is keen like a razor. I have prepared for this work. They don't even know what's coming."

Clarke stole a kiss and grabbed his hat off the hook. He thought he felt a tremble from Sandy but there was nothing more to say.

There was a murderer in his city who wasn't going to take a night off.

Neither would the Crimson Mask.

Detective Charles Norton stood on the steps of the City Morgue. He was of average height, a slim build and while he likely dressed smart enough reporting to work in the morning, now the sun was setting and his day must have been a long one. His tie was loose, the top buttons of his shirt were undone revealing his undershirt, and the hair that spilled out from under his hat was tussled.

Norton took a long drag off his cigarette and prepared to flick it into the gutter.

"I think the police should set an example, don't you Detective Norton?"

Norton spun, dropped the butt and reached for his service pistol.

"The Crimson Mask." Norton relaxed.

"At your service," Crimson Mask grinned.

"We've never met. How did you know who I was?"

"Your hat and attire fit the pay grade of a detective, you seem disheveled

enough to be struggling with a caseload that might vex even Sherlock
Holmes. I've read your file and my eyes on the inside told me what you
looked like."

"My back was to you."

"Even that cigarette can't mask the fumes that the city morgue sews into
your suit."

"Who else but cops go to the city morgue?"

"At this hour? None. But with a fresh corpse making three the number
of hits against the mob, I am the exception."

"Okay, fine, showoff. We don't need to talk about this out here where
any Tom, Dick and Harry can listen in. Follow me," Norton picked up his
butt and tossed it in the ashtray as he led the Crimson Mask inside.

"You have good reflexes, Detective."

"Alright, put a lid on it."

"Doctor Ed Furman, this is—"

"The Crimson Mask? Well, isn't that something?" Furman said.

The autopsy room looked as it always had to the Crimson Mask. Grey
tiles covered the floor and most of the wall. They seemed to suck the life
right out of him. The walls had seen a lot of death and there would be
countless more traveling beneath the off-white ceiling. It was a grim place.

The medical examiner was wearing hospital scrubs and thick black
gloves. He wore a well trimmed moustache and maintained a very neat
appearance. He smirked at the Crimson Mask.

"I'm helping the police with this string of murders."

"I gathered," Furman said, not unkindly.

"Any information you could give me would be helpful."

"I did just go over this with Detective Norton but, sure, I'm here anyway."

There was a body in the center of the sterile room under a lime green
sheet. The well manicured feet stuck out the bottom. One toe tagged.

"Meet George Alfani. Five foot nine, forty-nine years old, dark hair and
brown eyes. He was D.O.A. this morning. Cause of death is hypoxia due
to strangulation."

The Crimson Mask approached the body. What had Alfani done
wrong? Where had he gone? Why had he been targeted?

"A big man strangled him from the front using only his hands. That's
rare," the Crimson Mask said to no one.

"How do you know that?" Furman asked.

"You said hypoxia but there's no ligature marks and he doesn't seem to have drowned. The bruising on his neck could very easily be made by hands. It had to be a large man because there is a lot of fighting when someone is strangled. A man of equal size might fight free. Where was he found?"

"In his car, parked in front of his house," Norton supplied.

"Tell me about this scar." The Crimson Mask retrieved a magnifying glass from his coat and bent close to the forehead of the corpse.

It was another othala rune that had been cut into the forehead between the eyes.

"What's there to tell? It was done with a sharp instrument," Furman explained.

"Like a scalpel?" Norton guessed.

"The incision is too wide. This was done with a very sharp knife," the Crimson Mask clarified.

"Very impressive. You do your homework." Furman was very pleased with himself.

"What time was the body found?" the Crimson Mask inquired.

"Seven a.m. by the wife when she came out to get the morning paper. She found him lying in the front seat."

"She say where he had been?"

"No clue. He's out late three, four times a week." Norton said.

"Have you started questioning his crew?"

"Crew?" Furman blurted.

"Yeah, the word is he might be mobbed up. We're still looking into it," Norton replied.

"I'd like to hear what you learn, detective. Thank you for your time, Dr. Furman." The Crimson Mask headed for the door.

"Wait a minute, Mask. You knew he had a crew. What else do you know?" Norton followed the crimebuster.

"I know this is the third body in seven months and the police don't seem to be taking it very seriously."

"The mob is whacking their own. My bosses aren't exactly grief stricken. Still, I'm doing my job."

"You were right to call me, detective. Maybe your friends should ask themselves a few questions. Like what happens to those that get caught in such a crossfire? And who says this is the mob's handiwork?"

"What is that supposed to mean?" Norton stopped on the steps leading to the medical examiner's office.

The Crimson Mask neither broke pace or turned around as he descended. "When have the mob ever autographed their murders, detective?"

The sun set an hour earlier. The rich, criminal and otherwise, were out but not like a Saturday night when the spirits flowed and could be smelled on the streets from the speakeasies. The Diamond Club was a high end joint that catered to anyone that had money. Rumor was that the Mayor came in from time to time. Certainly Hollywood's greatest and the underworld's worst came often. It was part of the draw. You could rub elbows with some kind of famous if you went to the Diamond Club. There, everyone shined.

It was a good place for the Mask to troll for information. He had to create a different disguise for each visit but that was no bother. The chase and the performance therein was all part of the challenge.

The Mask wore an expensive jacket, some eyeglasses and a black tie. He had his shoes highly shined on the way over to the club. A gorilla of an usher eyeballed him, hesitated, then opened the door.

"Thank you, my man," the Crimson Mask said using an upper crust New England accent and tipped his hat.

The gorilla grunted.

The band pounded the walls with their horns as soon as the Mask entered the high ceiling foyer. Some well dressed guests mingled nearby. A woman dressed like a flapper let her eyes wash over the Crimson Mask. When she smiled, barely, she turned back to her group of male admirers. *Just another face in the crowd,* the Crimson Mask thought and continued into the main room.

The tables were filled to half capacity and he counted two scantily clad women selling cigarettes. The bandstand looked as if it could have fit more players as well. Perhaps it was the string section's night off. The bar was almost full. As he was alone he knew it would draw too much attention to take a table. Best to start at the bar and see what doors opened from there.

The Mask pulled out a silver cigarette case, popped it open and removed one. He sat at the bar, popped open his lighter and struck the fuse in one snap. He inhaled deeply.

"What can I get you, sir?" the bartender asked.

The bartender's moustache was pencil thin, his slick hair greased to complete order. Even if he wasn't taller than everyone he served his demeanor screamed condescension.

"What's interesting tonight?"

"You'll have to be more specific, sir."

"The strongest thing you have to sell, my man."

"Certainly, sir."

The Crimson Mask looked down the bar. There were a lot of coffee drinkers, some tea and a soda pop. It was possible that their drinks were laced with something stronger but who knew what the code words were to get things like that. Maybe after a few weeks of sneaking little sips of the dangerous stuff he might be trusted to get into the speakeasy. There was no time for the safe approach.

The bartender, his hair still perfect, his not so subtle loathing of the clientele still heavy in the air, returned carrying coffee on a saucer.

"Coffee?"

"From deep within the deserts of the middle east, sir. I'm sure you'll find it strong enough for your tastes."

"Well, that's fine, my good man, very fine indeed. But I fear you misunderstood me." He motioned for the bartender to bend closer. "I was thinking of something that only a man like my friend Tommy Gagliano might imbibe to warm his bones."

The bartender locked his gaze on the Mask and as if on cue the band finished their song.

"*You* are a friend of Mr. Gagliano?"

"Tommy and I go way back. Why, is he here tonight?"

"Mr. Gagliano is in. Would you like me to let him know you're here?"

"Indeed. Tell him Mr. Jawnhol is here for him."

The tender nodded once and stepped away to a telephone that sat centered in front of the vast mirror behind the bar. He dialed one number. His back was to the Mask but he cupped his hand around the voice piece so the Mask had no idea what was being said thanks to the band striking up again. The tender nodded twice and hung up.

"I'll take one of those cigars as well now that you're back," the Mask said.

The tender returned with a large cigar, clipped off the tip and handed it to the Mask. Once it was in the Mask's mouth, the tender produced a wooden match as if by magic and lit the cigar.

The Mask inhaled hungrily. "You know what, fella? I've been out of town for a long time but I knew a man named George that used to enjoy a good cigar almost as much as me. We came in here often enough, perhaps you know him. George Alfani?"

The tender blinked. "Certainly, he is often a guest of Mr. Gagliano."

"Tell him Mr. Jawnhol is here for him."

"Right, is he here tonight? My friend Georgie?"

"I have not seen Mr. Alfani tonight. However, you may see Mr. Gagliano now." The tender looked beyond the Mask's shoulder.

The Crimson Mask turned to look to his left and saw the well dressed gorilla from the front door standing behind him. His head was shaved clean. He didn't have much for eyebrows even. He was easily six inches taller than the Crimson Mask and had him beat by fifty pounds.

"Come with me," the gorilla said.

"Excellent." Puffing away on the cigar, the Mask followed.

They walked the length of the dance floor and through the seating area complete with high end table cloths and expensive crystal. More than one woman acknowledged the Mask as he traversed the floor. He responded with a nod or a smile. Some of the men saw him flirting and did not approve. All part of the act. The more people that saw him and remembered him the more witnesses that cops could use if things didn't go according to plan.

The bouncer had nothing to say. He didn't even turn to check and see if his guest was following. Perhaps he was used to people doing what they were told.

They did not head for the elevators or the stairs. Instead they turned off the dining room rug and went into the kitchen. The usher held the door a second after he went inside. The Mask followed. He took note of the myriad smells and mouth watering sights the chefs were concocting. The clientele will eat well tonight, the Mask thought. He was thankful that the clacking and chopping and slamming of large pans from the oven hid his growling stomach. He recalled eating breakfast, working through lunch and then cancelling dinner with Sandy. He regretted having to do that. The Mask didn't like excluding his long-standing teammate. But who he was dealing with was still a big fat question mark. Until the Crimson Mask understood the nature of the beast he would hunt alone.

"Excuse me, my man, but where *are* you taking me? I don't recall ever going this way in the past." The Mask blew a few smoke doughnuts in the air.

The big oaf stopped and faced him. "We're almost there," he growled.

"Excellent." The Mask grinned. "Everything smells wonderful! Keep up the good work!" the Crimson Mask shouted.

The usher stood at a metal door with an exit sign glowing over it. He swung the door open and held it.

"Outside? What is going on here? I am not some—"

"Yer gonna move, right now, without makin' a friggen sound, pal," a throaty voice whispered in the Mask's ear.

A new player in the game.

The statement was punctuated by a quick stab with something sharp to the Crimson Mask's lower back. The guide grinned and held the door open wider.

"Oh, certainly." The Mask wore a fearful look and quickly stepped to the open door.

The alley beyond the kitchen is perfect for the work at hand, the Crimson Mask thought. Two truck bays for deliveries, tall building opposite the Diamond Club, alley dead ends here. Truckers have to back in and there is space to turn around and get out. Two dumpsters and a smattering of worthless pallets.

A strong hand shoved him between the shoulder blades and the Mask went sprawling. He took his time getting up.

The metal door that led to the kitchen clanked shut.

"Hope it don't rain 'til we get done here," number two said.

"I'm goin' back to the door so it don't matter much to me. Let's do this."

Goon number one approached the Mask sitting in a modified Indian-style position.

"Who are you and what do you want to see Mr. Gagliano for?"

"We go way back, I thought it was time to catch up."

The bruiser bent down and picked up the Mask by the lapels, easily.

"Last chance, meatball. Then things get bloody."

The Mask mumbled something. The gorilla pulled the Mask's face down to his.

"Missed that, buddy?"

Agony burst through the thug's head when the Mask clapped both hands over his ears. He screamed, the Mask dropped to the ground, landed on his feet, and kicked the inside of the fellow's knee with a satisfying crack. The stooge fell howling. The Mask fired a kick to the man's head and he quit making noise.

The second tough raised his eyebrows and started his approach.

"You ain't bad," he conceded.

"You can always surrender and speed this along for me."

A butcher knife and a cleaver appeared in the man's hands. He smiled at the Crimson Mask.

"Couldn't afford a gun?"

"Always preferred blades," the man began hacking away.

The Mask gave ground for three swipes then dashed and jabbed. The knife-man's nose snapped satisfactorily.

"Son of a bitch!" The slasher attacked with fervor.

The blade-man would be getting black eyes from the nose break eventually. In the short term he was losing his vision. The Crimson Mask knew eyes tear up after a busted nose. The man was a street brawler with no discipline. He compensated the lack of sight with sheer ferocity and sloppiness. The Crimson Mask teased and dashed until the knife fighter was wheezing, then landed a kick to the gut that doubled him over. That set him up for the roundhouse punch behind the ear that slowed him, and an easily placed chop to the base of the skull ended the fight.

The Mask's jacket came off and he turned it inside out. It was modified to appear to be two coats if a quick-change was needed. The moustache was discarded and the glasses pocketed. He changed his tie and took the 1911 semi-automatic off the slumbering bouncer. He wasn't about to chance running into another weapons man unarmed. It wasn't his .38 but it would do.

Out of a secret pocket from his customized jacket he pulled the red, velvet domino mask and put it on. Once his hat was situated at a dynamic angle he opened the door and entered the kitchen.

The Diamonds Club was two stories and most of the action was on the first floor. The Mask hoped it wouldn't take too long to find out where Gagliano's office was. It only took a minute of looking to find a stairwell. There were some astonished stares and mumblings from the kitchen staff but no one tried to stop him. That was another perk of having a reputation. Most didn't know if he worked for the mob or against them but no one was willing to take the chance on guessing wrong.

The second floor door swung open as the Crimson Mask was about to reach for the knob. There stood an average looking goon in size and looks. He was still inhaling to voice some kind of objection when the Mask drilled him in the stomach then smashed his knee into the man's face. The Mask took the clip from the soldier's 1911 and dashed into the hallway. It didn't seem like this floor was terribly busy when the club was bouncing downstairs. The Mask took out who was likely the errand-boy. If he was lucky there would be only a man or two left to keep Gagliano safe.

Down the hall there was a sign on a door that read Tommy Gagliano.

"Convenient," the Mask knocked three times, hard.

"Who the hell is it? Bobby, were my instructions not clear?"

The Mask mumbled something incoherent. When the door started to open the Crimson Mask kicked in. The door cracked when it struck the red-headed heavy on the other side. He went stumbling backwards. A second man jumped up out of a chair.

The Mask was faster on the draw.

"Do it and I'll burn you down, Bruno," the Crimson Mask said.

The hood snarled and went for the piece. The Mask plugged him twice and marched into the room. Bullets tore through the door. The Mask dove to the floor and rolled. Another round came through the wall narrowly missing his shoulder. The maniac was still shooting from inside the office though he wasn't certain where the Mask was. Thankfully the hallway was vacant.

Laying on his belly, the Mask rolled. A bullet cracked into the floor where he had been. He leveled his gun six inches off the floor and started shooting from left to right through the wall. On the third shot he heard a scream and a thud. He rolled to the right, then to his back and ejected the empty clip, reloaded and finished rolling so his head and shoulders were through the doorway into the office.

A middle aged blond man sat on the floor tenderly examining his bleeding ankle. The revolver sat within arms reach and all but forgotten. His eyes widened at the site of the Mask aiming a pistol at him. The blonde looked at his gun, snarling.

"Be smarter than your hatchetman, Gagliano!"

"Crimson Mask! You bastard!" Gagliano cursed.

The Mask hopped to his feet, picked up Gagliano by the coat and slammed him onto his large wooden desk. He kicked the gun away without looking.

"What the hell do you think you're doing?"

"I'm here for answers, Gagliano."

"Answers? For what? I ain't tellin' you—"

The Crimson Mask back-handed the mobster.

"You'll talk. Look at you, you're dying to talk. Tell me about the killings!"

"It's a dangerous city, Mask. People get killed all the time."

The Mask gripped Gagliano by the injured ankle. Gagliano howled.

"Loud music downstairs. No one is going to hear you. No one is coming. Who killed Tommy Rheina, Pinzola and Alfani?"

Gagliano screamed and grabbed for his bleeding ankle. The Mask took him by the throat and squeezed.

"Okay... okay... I killed Rheina."

"You? Why? To move up?"

"Masseria was at war with Maranzano. Rheina was Masseria's partner in all kinds of stuff. Some things I wasn't even supposed to know about. Masseria kept squeezing us for money to take down Maranzano. Rheina got tired of it. We were our own gang; we didn't need him, but Masseria was more powerful.

"Rheina was sick of losing money to that horse's ass Masseria. He started talking about going over to Maranzano. Backing *him* over Masseria. So I saw my chance and I told Masseria about Rheina's idea. Even knew how to get rid of Rheina."

"Then you'd be in charge of the Rheina gang. What's a little murder among friends, right?" the Crimson Mask said.

"Rheina was a cheap bastard that took no risks. We could be making two or three times the cabbage if I was running things."

"So you had him killed."

"Right. Then that lying bastard Masseria put one of *his* guys in charge! In charge of *my* gang! The nerve of that wop bastard!"

"Why didn't you kill him?"

"It woulda cost too much. We hadn't found all of Rheina's stashes yet and hits like on a boss ain't cheap," Gagliano explained.

"You hired outside the gang for the killing?"

"Course I did. I didn't want it traced back to me. Plus maybe the next guy gets the idea that this is how things are done and I'm whacked next. Screw that and screw you, I need a doctor!"

"So Masseria pushes Pinzola on you and you can't stand the looks your guys are giving you, right? Like you got no stones? So you hire your guy to kill Pinzola to save your rep and slap Masseria in the face," the Mask repeated.

"You're goddamn right I did!"

"What about Alfani? What the hell did he do?"

"I never ordered no hit on George."

"Lying is a waste of my time, Tommy. He was marked like the other two. A rune was carved into him. The same killer did Alfani." The Crimson Mask gave the ankle a squeeze.

Gagliano screamed but looked more angry than scared.

"You got nerve callin' *me* liar! *You* whacked him!" Gagliano roared.

"Make sense, why would I kill Alfani?"

"He came in here the night you broke into in the ice house. He was madder than hell and running his mouth about you and how you think you run the town. How you got no right questioning anybody about business that ain't yours."

"And for that reason you thought I would come back and kill him?"

"You sayin' you didn't?"

"Hush!" The Crimson Mask tilted his head and listened. Had he heard something outside in the hall?

The first bullet took out the window behind the large desk. The impacts began tracking towards Gagliano who lay still, plugging his ears. It was a tommy-gun. The Crimson Mask immediately began drawing his borrowed 1911. Gagliano took two rounds before the Mask could return fire. His second shot hit the shooter in the left bicep and ending the spraying. The Crimson Mask heard the killer racing away and stopped shooting.

The Mask checked Gagliano's injuries. He was shot three times in the chest.

"You hold on, Gagliano. This isn't over."

"It is for me, Mask. Never shoulda ordered the hit with people I don't know."

A wracking cough overtook Gagliano. Foaming blood came out of his mouth.

"...grease ball grifter...little Tony... said they was good for two... just two," Gagliano closed his eyes and stopped breathing.

The Crimson Mask ran. He had only a general direction for the shooter but it was better than nothing. He turned left in the hall and noticed the blood on the wall from when he shot his target. It continued on the floor. The trail led all the way to the end of the hall to the stairs. The Mask gripped the metal door handle and began to ease it open. It seemed unlikely that the shooter would wait in ambush. He was injured and alone, the Mask hoped.

It took much control to tame a machine-gun and put the bullets where they're aimed. The Crimson Mask looked through the open door and noticed a faint crimson line. Slowly he shoved the door wider. It instantly occurred to him that the almost invisible red wire tied to the doorknob was a trip-line.

The Crimson Mask dove to the hall floor as the explosion blasted the door open and knocked him off his feet.

Head ringing and on rubbery legs the Mask got up. The walls facing the door were peppered with shrapnel. The Mask drew his gun and entered the stairwell. Covered in dust was the trail. The blood trail was bright and in larger splattering. The shooter had gone up the stairs to the roof.

There was no a bobby-trap on the roof door. The Mask eased out gun first. His target wasn't hard to spot. The shooter was laying near the roofs edge with his Thompson still clutched in his hands. He was the fastidious bartender that sold him a drink and a cigar less than a half hour earlier.

The man was dead. One of the Mask's shots must have hit an artery. There was a lot of blood around the body. The Crimson Mask searched the body for some kind of clue, some hint as to the man's identity. Whistling from the alley street below drew his attention.

The Mask looked over the edge of the roof. There was a Lincoln Model K parked near a side entrance. A large, barrel-chested man holding another Thompson aimed the gun up at the Crimson Mask.

"Damn it! The Crimson Mask!" he shouted.

"We're on it." Two other men in suits and hats that the Mask not seen materialized and headed for an entrance door. The big man chambered a round and prepared to fire.

The Crimson Mask fell back. Chips of brick and mortar peppered him like a hand grenade as the Thompson did its best to eat through the wall. The Crimson Mask found his footing, grabbed the bartender's machine-gun and raced for the door. Those other two were on their way up. No reason not to meet them half way. The Mask descended the stairs two at a time.

How was the bartender involved? Did Gagliano know he was the killer? He was *a* killer, maybe not *the* killer. Those three mooks outside were in with him somehow. *If what Gagliano said was the truth, that he knew nothing about Alfani getting killed, and I didn't kill him, why are they still wasting trigger men?*

"Hey, Mask!" Someone yelled from the floor below.

The Crimson Mask froze on the second floor landing.

"Give yourself up and we can do this quick," the man had a southern accent. North Carolina, the Mask thought.

"Really?"

They were still ascending the stairs, not waiting for an answer.

The Mask took off his hat and waved it over the eye of the stairwell. Two shots rang out. He could hear them ricocheting on the ceiling and higher stairs. The Crimson Mask fired a quick burst from the Thompson down the stairwell and ran through the hole that used to hold the second floor door. He wasn't about to exchange bouncing bullets with two shooters. The odds were not in his favor.

The Mask raced down the hall trying to make it to the other stairwell he had spotted earlier. He was thankful that he kept himself conditioned for moments like this. He almost made it to that second stairwell when one of the gunmen appeared in the doorway.

This one was dressed in an expensive suit and hat. He raised his machine-gun and with a grin, opened fire. The Crimson Mask returned fire as he dove to the right for the nearest office. He got to his feet and stuck his weapon into the hall and fired blindly. There was cursing and some return shots but not from the second stairwell.

His arm burned as a bullet hit his shoulder. The first hood had arrived on the second floor. The Mask took the machine-gun in his right hand and fired blindly down the left side of the hall. There was more cursing.

His machine-gun was empty. It had a straight magazine that held only twenty rounds. The two trigger men had fifty round drums locked in. They likely had a spare as well. Trying to hold them off would only result in his death.

The Crimson Mask hastily took in his surroundings. Gagliano lay on the desk as before. Almost exactly as before. In his red, wet hand he held his little black book. Who on earth was he trying to call, the Mask wondered? He reached for the book then froze. Two grenades rolled into the office.

There was only one door and death waiting beyond it.

He had seconds. The Mask pocketed the little black book and heaved the massive desk on its side and dropped behind it. The ensuing blast cracked the wooden top of the desk.

The Crimson Mask slid open the now smashed window behind the desk and took a deep breath.

"What the hell?" Someone in the corridor yelled.

"Open fire!" Another shouted.

The Crimson Mask looked out the window. The world record for the long jump is almost thirty feet, the Mask thought. He doubted he could come close to that and was thankful that he didn't have to. The dumpster in the alley was only half that distance. Besides, there was no other option.

Plaster and brick exploded around the Mask as he pushed off the window sill with everything he had. Overshooting the mark was also a concern briefly but the Mask found that he measured the distance perfectly. Had it been later in the night there might be more trash to cushion the landing. Bruising beats dead, he thought.

One of the shooters stuck his head out the window. The Crimson Mask had his 1911 out and fired. Cursing, the man ducked back inside. The Mask jumped out of the dumpster and eased himself behind it.

He heard the Thompsons firing and the bullets ricocheting and something more.

Sirens.

Someone must have heard the ruckus and called the boys in blue.

"You are done, Mask! You hear? You are the target now!" the man spoke with a southern accent but different from the dead man on the roof. This one sounded subdued like maybe it was something learned later in life.

The men argued but the Mask couldn't hear what was said. He wasn't about to stick his head out just in case it was a ruse. He could sit patiently until the police arrived.

"They're almost done evacuating the building, detective," the patrolman told Detective Norton.

"Fine, good," Norton said, "So what do you think, Mask? You gonna make it or what?"

"I don't think the bullet hit anything vital, Norton. I will need to head to the hospital, however."

"Fine, good. You wanna give me the fast version of what the hell went down here?"

"It's very simple. I am following the trail that you set me on."

"You thought the guy that killed the mob goons was in there? Safe bet, every trigger man in the city stops in here at one time or anther. Is that him on the roof?"

"No. You'll confirm this when you check his hands against the bruising on the bodies. He isn't nearly big enough." The Crimson Mask lit a cigarette.

"Wait a sec!" Norton jogged to the ambulance drivers pushing a gurney. He motioned over his shoulder for the Crimson Mask to follow him.

"That's Gagliano all right," the Crimson Mask confirmed.

"I figured. That look familiar?" Norton pointed to the corpse's right cheek.

The othala rune was cut into Gagliano's face.

"They must have done it after I jumped through the window." The Mask exhaled smoke through his nose.

"Yeah, they told me you took a dive. Two guys with tommy-guns and throwing grenades. You don't mess around when you start looking under rocks, do you?"

"There are murders being executed under strange circumstances with undeniable skill in our city, detective." The Crimson Mask walked away from both cop and corpse.

"The brass thinks its some nut job that's into mythology. Someone the mob pissed off with a grudge. They ain't listening to me. I got no manpower."

The Crimson Mask turned around, dropped his cigarette butt and stepped on it.

"Your bosses are way off. These people are anything but crazy. It's corruption like this that makes the Crimson Mask needed more than ever."

"Corruption? I don't think I like what you're implying."

"You're a good cop, Norton. Secure your crime scene. It's not you I don't trust. It's the greed of people in power. Stay inside the lines and you'll be fine."

The Crimson Mask could feel Detective Norton's eyes on him as he walked off.

The Crimson Mask closed the motel door and locked it. He stood and listened but heard nothing and went to the bed. He unpacked the emergency medical kit he carried in the trunk of his car and got to work. The bullet had passed through the meat of his shoulder. The Mask hadn't heard the shooter enter the hall behind him. The shooter was good. All his attackers were. It confirmed his suspicions.

How many were in this crew? Was he followed to the motel? He drove around for an hour watching for a tail and weaving through traffic as safely as possible. The Mask wanted to call Warrick or Dave, and certainly Sandy. The government might not be the only ones that know how to wiretap a phone though. One slip and his hunters might learn his location or that of whomever he was contacting.

The Mask applied a fresh dressing to his shoulder and took some aspirin.

He dragged a cigarette from the pack and sparked a match to life with his thumbnail. It tasted good.

The Crimson Mask flipped through the little black book again. He already read it but nothing jumped out at him. Gagliano was holding onto it with his last ounce of strength. Was it a dying man's last act to comfort himself or something else? Did he regret calling down firepower that had clearly gotten out of hand? Was there a message in the act?

"What are you trying to tell me?" the Mask asked the book, "What *did* you tell me?"

The Crimson Mask closed his eyes and drew on his near perfect memory.

"You're a good cop, Norton. Secure your crime scene."

"...grease ball grifter...little Tony... said they was good for two... just two," the Mask said in a perfect reproduction of Gagliano's voice.

The Mask thought the first half of the rambling was referring to one or two people. More likely one. If it was one person then—given Gagliano's race, use of a nickname and the fact that Anthony or Tony is a popular name among the Italian community—he was likely referring to an acquaintance. The mask thumbed through the book again. There were twelve entries that had the name Anthony or Tony in them. Three shared the surname Gagliano.

The Mask decided to start with the family. The first number was disconnected. The second was the widow of the late Alberto Gagliano. The Mask dialed the last of the 'family Tony's.'

"75th Ranger Regiment, Charlie Company Barracks, CQ desk. Corporal Widner Speaking," a bored voice said.

"Is this an army fort?" the Crimson Mask asked.

"Very funny. Who is this? I gotta keep this line clear."

"Maybe I got the number wrong. Is this Fort Hood?" The Crimson Mask used the name of the only army base he could think of. Fort Hood was in Texas but he aimed for sounding like a confused caller.

"No," the man laughed, "This is Fort Benning. Georgia?"

"There are so many numbers here. He gets transferred around a lot. Sorry for the trouble. I'm looking for a Tony Gagliano. You might know him by Little Tony?"

"Yeah, I know Corporal Gagliano. Who can I say is calling?" the corporal asked.

"Tell him it's his Uncle Tommy from back home." The mask eased into the Tommy Gagliano accent.

"Just a minute, sir."

It took longer than a minute for the sound of boots on waxed floors to return to the phone.

"Yo, Tommy? That you?" a young man said.

"Tony, how they treating you down there at Benning?" the Crimson Mask said.

"Not bad. Kinda late to be callin' though. I was about to—"

"Nevermind what you was about to do, you dumb bastard. You got a lot to answer for."

Silence.

"What... what are you talking about, Uncle Tommy?"

It was *uncle Tommy* now. The kid was scared of Gagliano even though he's an Army Ranger. What kind of hold did Tommy have on him?

"...said they was good for two... just two," the Mask recited.

Tony sounded like he was cupping the phone in case anyone else was around. "That was the deal. They did that first thing and then later you called them back. What's the problem? They screw the pooch or something?" Tony whispered.

"You're goddamn right they did! They ain't stopping! How do I shut 'em down!"

"How the hell should I know? I talked to my guy like I said. They showed and talked to you and did whatever you told 'em to."

There was fear in Tony's voice. The Mask knew he had him.

"They're killing *our* people now, Tony. My family! Who the hell *are* these guys?"

"I dunno! I never met 'em . They're from on-base I figure, maybe Rangers or regular infantry. I swear I don't know, Uncle Tommy."

"You just wait for my call, you hear me, Tony? I got a mess to clean up, but when I'm through maybe I'll come down south and we'll have us a talk, right?"

The only response was muted breathing.

"Be seein' ya, Little Tony."

The Mask hung up.

"Rangers."

The Crimson Mask had been chipping away at the mob since he first donned the mask. Masseria, the Mask had learned, had his hands in a little of everything. Prostitutes, protection rackets, he robbed the shipyards and never stopped being hungry. The big money was in selling hooch and running speakeasies. There was no way to keep track of where all the illegal booze joints were from week to week. The police would shut one down and the next night three more would open. As a rule the Mask generally left them alone. Those places were great for gathering information in a number of disguises. The police and Bureau of Investigation could chase whiskey drinkers. There were far more important criminals to hunt down.

Ex-Rangers plying their trade as freelance assassins topped that list. The Mask should not have been surprised that soldiers his country trained would turn on those they were to protect.

Everything that the Mask knew about Army Rangers he had learned from reading history books and there wasn't much there on tactics. What he lacked in definitive information he made up for in other areas. He knew a lot about strategy and had studied some of history's greatest leaders. He had to assume that the Rangers covered some of the same information in their training. All he could do was guess and act based on the information at hand and his instincts.

It had always worked in the past.

He had never faced elite soldiers murdering in his city before.

It seemed logical, given the string of events that the ex-Rangers were trying to maintain invisibility. The killing of Rheina was practical for Masseria and Gagliano. Masseria double-crossed Gagliano and planted Pinzola in the leadership of the Rheina gang. Gagliano decided to take what was his and called his contact again. The killers returned to New York. They did the second job then maybe saw an opportunity for even bigger money.

After the Pinzola hit they started gathering intelligence on the theater of war among the Italian mob. They then inserted themselves into the structure. The soldier playing bartender overheard Alfani running his mouth. The killers silenced him before any more could be spilled like who Alfani worked for and was likely abetting. That would have led someone to Gagliano. So Gaglaiano had to be killed. Once the contact was dead they cannot be traced back to the killers.

Or could they?

The Crimson Mask stepped out of an alley on 116th street. He wore a hobo disguise: feather-thickened padding around his midsection, holey clothes that stunk of cheap whiskey and cigar smoke, a beige long coat and an aged fedora that looked like a dog used it as a chew toy.

Masseria was still alive. He had Gagliano hire the ex-Rangers in the first place. If the Crimson Mask knew this then it figured they did as well. He risked a quick call to Warrick to learn that Masseria wasn't even hiding. His favorite place to eat was the Venezia Restaurant on East 116th Street in East Harlem, Manhattan.

Would the killers go for Masseria? Was there time for the Mask to save one life from their touch? Did the ex-Rangers think the Crimson Mask would try to save Masseria and sit in ambush like a spider for a fly? There was one way to find out.

The military called it recon. Short for reconnaissance. The Crimson Mask started reconnoitering the surroundings of the Venezia Restaurant from a mile out using a spyglass from rooftops.

Better think like a solider if you're going to catch one.

The Crimson Mask inhaled deeply on his cigar then coughed violently and staggered down 116th Street towards the East River. The big man had not moved since the Crimson Mask's initial reconnaissance of the area.

The only information the Mask possessed had come from Lil Tony Gagliano. They were either infantry or worse, Army Rangers. The Crimson Mask chose the better trained of the two: Rangers. It took the Mask two hours of spying, crawling, climbing and changing from one disguise to another to spot the four men that were trying not to be seen. They were all waiting for something that had not arrived in the time the Crimson Mask spent spying.

The man hiding in the shadows of an alley to the west of the Venezia Restaurant was easily missed until a passerby was within arm's reach of the giant. He had to be closer to seven feet than six; his cheap suit strained to keep his arms and chest covered. He was likely narcissistic, like many bodybuilders.

The Crimson Mask inhaled deeply from his cigar and exploded in a coughing fit that steered him into the alley. The brute dashed out of the way letting the Crimson Mask crash into the wall. He leaned on the wall heavily trying to breathe.

"Get outta here, bum," the brute said.

The fellow kept himself between the 12 gauge shotgun he carried and the Mask. His boots were military issue.

"Sorry, sorry, gimmie a hand, hey?" the Crimson Mask slurred while falling into the man.

There wasn't time for him to avoid the incoming body. Reflexively the ex-soldier brought the shotgun around to ward off the incoming body. The Crimson Mask lashed out with the butt of his pistol and broke the guy's right thumb on the gun-butt, then twisted the shotgun away. Enraged eyes met the Mask's as the butt crashed into the side of the buiser's face, stunning him. A second blow took him in the back of the head and dropped him, dazed, to one knee.

"You're a strong one." The Crimson Mask took the shotgun with both hands and delivered a vicious butt-stroke to the head. The big man fell unconscious.

◆⟫━━ ● ┄┄┄ ● ━━⟪◆

The sniper on the roof of the used clothing emporium at the end of the block was the first soldier the Mask found when he began his sweep of the rooftops. He lay within a shadow. He wouldn't have been smoking if he thought anyone was going to be looking for him.

In twenty minutes the Mask had closed in until he was standing behind him. The sniper was looking down into the shaded back lot that businesses on both sides of the street shared. There was a man standing on the back step of the Venezia. *Strange that he's standing in the open,* the Mask thought.

The sniper rolled onto his back and swung the rifle around. The Crimson Mask jumped on top of him, the barrel scraped across his ribs under the Mask's arm. The sniper inhaled to call out and took a head-butt to the nose, silencing him. The Crimson Mask tore the rifle away and threw it out of reach.

A sharp pain flashed across the Mask's left shoulder. He rolled away and sprung to his feet. The sniper was also on his feet. He carried a knife in each hand.

A knife fighter? I was expecting guns more than anything else.

He could have just drawn his .38 and fired, but the report would have alerted the man on the stoop if the scuffling around hadn't already. The Mask drew his sap. They circled one another.

"You busted my nose, jerk," the sniper said.

"I'm not done, either," the Mask said.

Snarling, the sniper charged forward, one knife in a reverse grip, slashing in a wide arc and using quickly predictable patterns. After a series of back and side steps, the Mask presented his arm as an easy target and the sniper slashed. The Crimson Mask brought down the sap on the outstretched hand, ducked the second hand and cracked the sniper in the temple, the nose and the opposite temple.

The sniper stumbled back holding his nose and the Mask advanced. The knife slashed out again but the Mask caught his wrist and twisted. The Mask jerked the arm and felt the sniper's shoulder pop out of joint. The sniper grimaced and would have yelled but the Mask took his wind from him with a punch to the gut. A gun butt to the back of the head took consciousness from him.

He looked at the sniper's battle fatigues; they were dyed black. *The better for night work,* the Mask thought and grinned.

The Crimson Mask exited the alley and entered the quad. It was almost complete darkness except for the back stoop lights over the doors of various businesses. The ground was a series of concrete slabs that were anything but level. Years of allowing trees to grow and set their roots in the quad made a level walking plane impossible.

The third man stood sentry at the back door of the Venezia Restaurant. The Crimson Mask was dressed in the sniper's black fatigues and carried his rifle. He watched the sentry's head move from point to point, and when he had finished he started over again. The Mask saw no weapons but that didn't mean much. When the sentry's head was turned as far away as it was going to be, the Mask started limping forward. He leaned heavily on the rifle. He walked in the shadows for as long as possible so from a distance he might more resemble the sniper from the roof.

The sentry made him almost immediately.

"Stop right there," the sentry said and faced the Mask.

A pistol appeared in his hand but remained lowered at his side.

"Don't! It's me! The Crimson Mask is here. He caught me on the roof!" The Mask imitated the sniper's voice as best he could.

The mercenary pointed his gun. "Eight legs."

"What? Listen, the Crimson Mask could be anywhere." The Mask took a cautionary step.

"Last chance. Eight legs."

The first half of the phrase was 'Eight legs' and he expected the real sniper to have the proper response. The Crimson Mask silently cursed himself for not reasoning a military group would employ passwords. Something that had eight legs. A spider or an octopus would be too easy. Was it some kind of machinery? A maneuver for four men to use in combat? Perhaps something from Norse mythology?

The Crimson Mask simply did not know and time was a factor if he was going to get to Masseria before he tried to leave for the evening. Even the mob didn't work all night long.

He had one choice. He dropped the sniper rifle and held up his hands.

"You've got me. You caught the Crimson Mask."

"Damn right we did."

What was that old Marine Corps saying? Improvise, adapt and overcome ...

"As promised, Mr. Masseria, the Crimson Mask. Bound and defenseless," the guard proclaimed.

The Crimson Mask was quickly escorted from the rear, through the kitchen and into the dining area of the Venezia Restaurant. At the center table of the modest eatery sat 'Joe the Boss' Masseria and four of his mercenaries. There was one waiter, a bartender drying glasses, and the sentry with a gun digging into the Crimson Mask's spine.

"The spaghetti smells magnificent," the Crimson Mask said smiling.

"It is indeed, Mr. Mask is it?" Masseria said.

"Sometimes."

"I have to admire a man that makes a stand for what he believes in. You picked the wrong side, but then we can't all be right, now can we?"

The soldiers agreed rapidly like good yes-men.

"You think you're smart, Masseria?"

"Careful, Mask. I got a gun at your back."

"You think you do. But this bunch you have on the payroll, the out of town talent, isn't quite as obedient as you think," The Mask said, "I'm going to reach into my coat and grab a cigarette. Don't get twitchy, anybody."

"I searched him, relax," the gunman said.

Masseria looked irritated but concealed it well enough. The Crimson Mask slowly drew a cigarette out of a breast pocket of his borrowed fatigues and struck a match off his thumb to light it. After a long drag he exhaled the smoke.

"Not as obedient as you think and not as smart as they think they are. I've been on to these guys since Pinzola was ventilated. One of yours, right Masseria? You figured out that it was Gagliano before the modus operandi was revealed by the cops. That was nice; misleading the cops into thinking it was some kind of crazed maniac killing for some mythological ideology.

"The problem is your guys never take their boots off. Five distinctively military boot prints were easy to spot in the dust of the Pinzola crime scene. Another strangulation in the name of Odin? No, just a brute with a lot muscles. They were a little too precise, these guys. I guessed Rangers. Am I right?"

"Shut up. Why are we listening to this fool?" the man behind him snarled.

"Because it amuses me. No one has ever caught the Mask before and I'm enjoying this. Besides, I think you've got him covered," Masseria laughed.

"There was no need to kill Alfani just for talking to me. That was excessive and only made me more interested, frankly. I know he was part of your scheme. But Gagliano didn't care for that much, did he? Turned these vets on you, didn't he? On Pinzola anyway. Then you backed off. Left Gagliano in charge of his part of the family while you kept warring on Maranzano and milking the Rheina gang for profits.

"These guys were supposed to kill and walk but I think they had plans of their own. After collecting their paycheck from Rheina, they thought they could get some more money by switching to your team. How's this sounding so far, Joe?"

"Keep going, Mask," Joe lit a big cigar. "I'm enjoying this."

"You still got scared the cops might pick up the trail; especially after I talked to Alfani. Bye-bye Alfani, tragic victim of Odin's Killer. Then in case I caught Gagliano's name, you had your mole drop his cover and moved on him. I got there first and took out one of your boys. That wasn't supposed to happen was it?"

The Crimson Mask felt the gun barrel jab into his back. "Easy, pal. I'm getting to the good part."

"You better be, Mask," Masseria said.

"You'll love this, I promise. So your guys nail poor Gagliano, already down for the count and then come after me."

"Are you saying that you did not kill Tommy Gagliano?" Masseria look confused.

"Of course not, why would I? I had nothing on him. Did *they* tell you I did? And then what, *they* chased me off? Does that line up with what you've heard of me?

"So after they kill me, on your order, then what, they stick around as enforcers for you?"

Masseria had no answer.

"They offer to whack Maranzano and his crew for you? Five guys, even with your gunsels, against his army? Maybe they take your money and fail. Or claim to fail. Maybe they go and ask Maranzano if *he* can afford them. Your crew would be the easier target. I bet they already have. This set-up was *their* idea right? Five trained killers and you and your henchmen here? Who do you think will come out on top?"

"Five guys?" Masseria pointed at the man behind the Mask. "You said there was four. You got a fifth guy, Garrick? You screwin' around here?"

"I told you not to listen to this freak in a mask!" Former Sgt. Garrick, said.

"Answer me!"

Garrick did not.

"Why don't you ask the bartender?" the Crimson Mask said.

It happened in seconds.

The Crimson Mask stepped backwards, into Garrick, landed a fist to his groin, kicked a leg out from under him, grabbed his pistol with his right hand and slammed the man's head off the nearest table with his left. He pointed the gun at the bartender.

The bartender drew one gun from behind his back and aimed at the Crimson Mask. A second shot out of his sleeve and into his left hand. This was aimed at Masseria.

Two hoods drew guns on the bartender and the other two aimed at the Crimson Mask. Only Masseria was unarmed. He inhaled deeply from his cigar. There was no stress on his face.

"Never bring in outside talent. I know better, but I got a little greedy in all the excitement."

"You idiot, Masseria. Listening to some vigilante like the Crimson Mask. He is trying to drive us apart. Everything was working! The Mask is the enemy!" the bartender roared.

"I don't know you and I sure as hell don't trust your team." Masseria paused, "Boys, kill 'em all."

Gunfire erupted between both groups.

The Crimson Mask dropped to the floor. He flicked his cigarette butt into the eyes of the closest man aiming a gun at him. The gunman jerked reflexively as hot ash exploded in his eyes. His shot missed and his partner took a forearm to the face making him miss. Bullets found them both and they fell.

The bartender fired with both hands. The Mask kicked a table over. It took the worst of the gunfire but did little more than redirect the rounds coming at him. One burned his neck, another split his thigh open. The Crimson Mask fired twice, catching the bartender in the mouth and forehead. He turned his .38 automatic on the two others as they were recovering their senses and plugged each in the chest.

The other shooters sagged in their seats next to Masseria, dead. The bartender had been an excellent shot with both hands. The spring-loaded Derringer up his sleeve had spit lead twice; one had caught the crime boss along the side of his neck.

Masseria tried to appear calm but he was losing the battle.

The Crimson Mask got to his feet and checked his neck injury.

"I can't believe I ain't dead. How did you know the bartender was in on it?" Masseria asked.

"His haircut suggested it. His right hand disappeared behind the counter and stayed there. He cleaned the same section of the bar a dozen times once I entered the room. And he wasn't Italian, *Giuseppe*," the Crimson Mask said.

"What I don't get is why save me? I ain't on your side. You been bustin' my operations for years."

"If the police can't find anything to convict you with, you can expect me to continue giving you my attention for as long as it takes."

"You're crazy," Masseria said, "You're just one guy."

"I think I made a difference tonight, Joe, don't you? No need to answer now, I think the truth will come to you with all the time you are going to have to think in the slammer."

The Crimson Mask picked up the black phone on the bar and began dialing the police station. He was hurt but not spent and the job was done. He could take some time off knowing he did all he could have and it had paid off.

Doc Clarke worked at City Hospital tomorrow and so did one Sandy Gray.

Maybe she had some time to cash a rain check.

THE END

About This Tale

I had never even heard of the Crimson Mask before taking this gig for Airship 27. In fact, I think I almost named one of my pulp characters the Crimson Mask a few years ago. To be honest I've not written too many copyrighted characters. Couple that with the fact that it takes place in the 1930s and you have a whole world of research for this writer to find his voice for a tale of the Crimson Mask.

Good thing I love researching things.

I definitely come from a super hero, sci fi, horror, fantasy kind of place where everything is larger than life. Writing Doc Clarke, aka the Crimson Mask, a character very much rooted in reality, was going to be a challenge. While I like to watch films like *Magnum Force*, the Bourne trilogy and *Tears of the Sun*, films populated by mere if well-trained mortals, I didn't have a lot of experience *writing* them. I knew that Airship 27 had a very high standard of excellence for their tales and if I was going to make the cut I had better bring my A game.

The Crimson Mask stories I read in my research showed a man that was adept at fighting, smart in this sleuthing and clever in his use of disguise. What a horrible person to have on your trail! He can be anyone, mimic any voice, alter his appearance with ease and then beat you down once he gets in close. And you didn't even know he was there.

The police welcome his help. What a refreshing change from most of the vigilante stuff that I was used to reading. I enjoyed writing the scene where the Mask goes to the city morgue and chats with Detective Norton and the M.E. It seemed to me that, more often than not. The Mask is going to be the smartest man in the room. Even if he is not prepared, the man is good at thinking on the fly and I tried to write him as such.

In retrospect I think I should have included his trio of friends (Warrick, Small and Gray) more, but to be honest I didn't think the Mask would want them getting involved in such a dangerous game once the Mask knew he was up against ex-military types. While they are all dear and valued friends of his, it is for that reason that I didn't think he wanted them in harms' way. It seemed sound that he would risk the dangers himself to remove his friends from the equation.

Far and away most of my research went into details of the time period. I'm not from the U.S.A. so I missed a lot of the history that everyone here takes for granted. All my 1930s knowledge comes from documentaries and old movies, and who knows how accurate those are? Things like what guns were used then by cops and bad guys, who drove what kind of car, how much was a ham sandwich at a deli in Manhattan, did they have traffic lights yet, were there weight lifting competitions, the FBI was called simply the Bureau of Investigations and dozens of other tidbits. I sprinkled in some period sensitive slang in there, too, just for flavor. I pride myself on being as authentic as possible in my work (if it makes sense to the piece in question). What can I say, it is just part of the writer that I am.

Along those lines comes the plot. Tommy Gagliano, "Fat Joe" Pinzolo, Gaetano Rheina, Giuseppe "Joe the Boss" Masseria and Salvatore Maranzano are all real gangsters from this time period. I watch a lot of documentaries and I always pick up things here and there bouncing around the web. It didn't take a lot of effort to find a nook in New York of the 1930s underworld and spin my tale out of that point in history.

I served in the American military so I know about how some of the infrastructure works. Let's be honest: given what we know about the Crimson Mask, how many people are going to keep him on the run and guessing? I thought why not try some ex-military types? I knew Rangers and Infantry soldiers when I was in. Nothing like the five I created here. Rangers aren't known for being physically weak or immoral but they do fight a certain way and have been trained to fight a certain kind of battle. I thought that if I took the idea of *scum-bag* Rangers of the lowest moral character and aimed them at doing assassination work for the New York mob, I might just have a worthy foe for the Crimson Mask. (Time and reader response will tell if I succeeded.)

The Crimson Mask stands out to me from among most of the other crime busters of this period in that he isn't about the gun per se, he's not crazed but he is determined. He's dynamic in both mind and body. Outside of the mask he does right by his community and cares about the people. Sounds like a well balanced guy and strong lead for a crime-busting story.

I had a great time writing him in his New York and would love to do it again.

Thanks for reading.

C. WILLIAM RUSSETTE has had comic books *Lucifer Fawkes: Blood Flow* and *The Blind Ones* published through Rorschach Entertainment. In 2010 Pro Se Productions published a number of his short stories in Pro Se Press. In 2011 ALL-STAR PULP COMICS from Airship 27 Productions included a short Black Bat comic written by C. William Russette.

His blog can be found here: (http://dungeonwall.blogspot.com/).

He lives in Pennsylvania with his wife and son.

Carnival of Lost Souls
by J. Walt Layne

In New York City, on a cold drizzling night in the late winter of 1932, two years and a hundred city blocks from where Wall Street fell. Aside from the privileged few, this neighborhood was so poor they couldn't tell. It was here in the Bowery, at the end of Short Stooksbury Road, which isn't there anymore, in the nicest building in the neighborhood retired mobster Vincent Sorrento came home from a late card game to find his wife of forty years murdered.

Vincent had been at Aces in Hell's Kitchen. It was a small club, owned by Jack Fratelli. Jack was the son of his pal from the old days, the late Frank Fratelli. Aces was a bottle of Odd Duck on organized crime's top shelf. It was a legit joint. They served drinks and the cook didn't do short order, it was a dinner club. After hours Jack ran a small card game, mostly to allow friends of the old man to gather and be nostalgic. No family or company business was transacted under his roof. It was neutral territory, and cop friendly. But nobody messed with Jack.

Vincent had a couple of scotches, and played out the hundred he'd brought. On his final hand he'd had nothing and drew into a straight royal flush, the closest guy to him had an ace and a pair of sixes. Vincent knew when it was time to go. He gathered his winnings, paid the tab for the table, shook hands and walked home.

He turned his collar up and buttoned his coat against the constant rush of the sleet. The icy wind was cutting and he walked quickly. As he approached his building, a four flat brownstone that he owned and rented out to his three sons and their families, nothing felt out of place. The light was on in the kitchen window, a sure sign that Gracie was in bed. It was quiet on the street, save for the hail that would have drowned out the noise of marauding pachyderms.

Vincent turned the knob and the door was locked. He thought it was strange, but considering what had been in the papers lately, he fished in his pocket for the leather thong on which he'd strung keys for as long as he could remember. The last thing that crossed his mind as he pushed the key into the lock was how fresh and clean it smelled.

When he pushed open the door, the whoosh of warm air that rushed out to meet him carried a sickening putrid smell of coppery sulfur. Vincent's gut wrung itself out as fifty years of being a made man rushed through his mind's eye. He knew the smell of death, it was an unwelcome visitor.

"No!" he rushed in, leaving the door hang open, as he entered the living room. The smell of blood hung here like a dark veil. He switched on the light. Graciella Sorrento lay in the center of the large braided rug. She'd been garroted, and her hands severed. In her mouth was stuffed a brightly colored handkerchief. A short distance from her blackened face and bulging eyes sat a stoneware cookie jar, with the lid slightly tilted.

"No!" Vincent cried out. His soul cracked as his knees settled into the cooling, sticky wetness on the saturated rug. He got up quickly, pausing only at the roll-top desk for the small revolver that lay in the top drawer as he strode into the kitchen. Suddenly the last thing he'd have ever thought of crossed his mind. He tapped the cradle switch on the phone three times. "Operator, I—I need the police."

Queensborough, one week later, Alvin Baker was sleeping soundly. His wife switched on the light when the phone started to ring. Alvin went to the kitchen and picked up the receiver. "Yeah, do ya's have any idear what time it is?"

"Is this Alvin Baker?" An antiseptic male voice asked in a somber tone.

"Yes, this is Al Baker," Alvin replied, shaking his head a little and running a hand over his face, fighting sleep for consciousness.

"Mr. Baker, my name is Carl York. I'm a Sergeant with the 59th Precinct, Queensborough Police. I need you to come to your shop. I'll explain when you get here."

Alvin shuddered, as he remembered that cold, wet, windy night back in 1929 when he'd made the decision to reopen his parent's bakery on stolen funds. He and Edith had sunk every penny into the bakery when his financial firm had failed. He remembered the day it had happened very clearly. He'd gone to the bank to do his morning deposits and as he passed the newsstand on his way into the bank he heard the delivery man from the times tell the newsboy that the Manhattan Savings and Loan had defaulted and that there was a line two blocks long of people trying to get their money.

Alvin entered the bank and exchanged his deposit slip for a short form bulk cash receipt and withdrew all funds from his client service account.

He made it a point to speak to a number of people—a cashier, a teller, two assistants to the bank president—and shook hands with the manager when he got up to leave.

He had promptly taken the money to his office and locked it in the safe. Within days thirty banks had defaulted. His clients were starting to ask questions and he assured them that everything was fine. When he arrived home, his wife delivered the friendly news that all of their personal accounts were frozen and for all intents and purposes they were financially ruined.

His mind raced. They went through their financials and found their single unencumbered asset, a small neighborhood bakery that had been his mother and father's retirement dream to turn his mother's craft of baking into an income to fund their elder years. After they both passed away in 1927, Alvin had left the bakery closed but intact, lacking the nerve to actually part with his parents' dream. He found the key to the bakery in a jar full of forgotten hardware in the cellar.

On the next day of particularly foul weather, he'd taken all of the money from the safe at his financial concern and set the office ablaze. He disappeared into the night, stopping briefly at the bakery to hide the money in the much smaller floor safe. He arrived home and was in bed before his wife and son had arrived from the train station.

They'd no sooner set their bags down, when there was a knock at the door. A policeman and the precinct fire chief were there, asking to speak with Alvin. Though he was not a gifted liar, he convinced them that he'd closed the financial office earlier in the afternoon because of the weather and had been home all night.

When Alvin arrived at the bakery, his stomach sank as he remembered the one detail of the night he started down the road to hell, which he'd managed to forget.

The fire in the bakery had been contained to the lower kitchen. Aside from smoke, and some cracked plaster there was little actual fire damage. The heat and explosive sound had likely been caused by a back draft that had blown the fire out. The question on the minds of the police was, how?

The fire inspector surmised that in some unrepeatable way that there had been a dust explosion, possibly caused by an open flame and an unimaginable quantity of dust created by flour in the air.

When the police officer led Alvin into the bakery, at first the only apparent damage was from smoke, at the top of the walls. But then they led him through the main kitchen to the stairs and down into the lower kitchen, where between the prep tables, which had been arranged in the same fashion as the desks in his financial office, lay Charles Baker, Alvin's only son. As his heart broke he remembered the charred body of his clerk, Mitch Curry who had entered the office to try and put out the fire. A short distance away from Charles's body was a small wooden pin, like a club that a juggler might use.

Broadway, a few weeks on, time was drawing nigh on the eve of April Fool's Day. Bob Clarke and Sandra Gray rolled into the lot at the Cohan Theater. They planned to take in the final curtain of *Dim the Lights on Broadway*, the final George M. Cohan production starring Gisela Margoles, the burlesque performer turned starlet, discovered by none other than Cohan himself.

Astrid Minx, a rising starlet and school chum of Sandra Gray, met the happy couple just inside the theater lobby and invited Sandra and her very significant other backstage to meet the show's most esteemed producer, Mr. George M. Cohan. She was also girlishly interested in Sandy's opinion of her somewhat steamy beau, Tom O'Donnell, whom Bob recognized as the notably nefarious adult child of new money. Tom's father found his wealth by stabbing a hard working gas driller in the back. Quite literally, though nonesuch could be proved.

After introductions to George and Mary Cohan, and watching part of Gisela's libretto from backstage, Astrid led them to a dressing room with a large gold star on the door, and a walnut plaque bearing the name Astrid A. Minx. After an exchange of encouraging appellation and snickering guffaws Astrid flung open the door saying, "I hope you like my Tom. He always waits for me in my dressing room." A moment later she let out a blood-curdling scream.

Astrid's boyfriend, the man-child formerly known as Tom O'Donnell, dressed in formal attire, was seated in a very cheap wooden folding chair at a tiny rustic military style field desk. A geological survey map of the OH-PENN natural gas range was spread across the small desktop. O'Donnell's throat had been cut with a broken champagne bottle, the jagged neck of which had been stabbed into his back with such force that it stuck and stood upright.

Astrid collapsed, fainting straight away. If Doc Clarke hadn't caught her she'd have slammed into the floor. He and Sandra helped Astrid onto the couch in the hallway and Cohan called police. Something about this scene didn't jibe, Bob felt an odd familiarity but nothing he could put a finger on. Sandra and Astrid were likewise puzzled by their macabre discovery.

Bob spent meticulous minutes within the scene searching for clues until the police arrived. Through channels administered by long time friend, former police commissioner Ted Warrick, he planned to obtain information on all recently filed cases that were ruled homicide.

Cohan, more than a little upset, and rightfully so, agitated Clarke and then Police Sergeant Paul Garret, a recently promoted import from Queens by saying, "How am I supposed to have a show with a dead body in my ingénue's powder room?"

"Don't look now, Mr. Cohan, but your sweet Miss Innocent is down for the count on the fainting couch," the cop quipped with equal veracity.

"Look sonny boy, you manage the stiff, and let me worry about show business, my little Minx is doing what an ingénue is supposed to do, just not on cue." Cohan's animated animosity would have been comic if not for the ferocity of it. The message was quite clear: 'dead bodies are bad for business so make this one go away.'

At the end of the evening, Sandy drove Bob into lower Manhattan, three blocks from the East River. She nosed the game little roadster into the curb at the dimly lit corner of East Avenue at Carmody Street. Bob, or Robert Clarke, Ph.G., Doc Clarke as he was known in the neighborhood, or in his less than frequent work at City Hospital, was beloved in the neighborhood for the giving nature of his business.

The drug store was a front for the Crimson Mask's secret lair. Inside he discovered his friend and assistant, Dave Small, cleaning up and restocking. He was also quite surprised to find Ted Warrick frantically pacing near the counter of the closed store.

"Ted, what are you…? Never mind, I was going to call you anyway. Tonight while we were at the theater, a body was discovered in Astrid Minx's dressing room. Something about the scene was familiar, but didn't belong," Bob said quickly.

"Yes, when I heard I came right over," Ted replied, and started for the back room.

"You mean more out of place than a dead body?" Dave remarked as he locked the door and turned out the main lighting.

"Dave, Astrid is a friend. We only got to go to Mr. Cohan's show because she got us tickets. The performance was sold out."

In the back room, which served as the Crimson Mask's secret lab, Bob Clarke set an enameled coffee pot over a Bunsen burner and placed the percolator basket inside. The group sat around a small lab table and Bob explained to Ted what they'd discovered.

"You say that inside the dressing room Tom O'Donnell was found dead with his throat cut at a staged crime scene." Bob and Sandy both nodded, "Well, then it should come as no surprise to you that this is not the first such case discovered in the city. About a month ago now, maybe six weeks, cops in Queens filed a strange report on a bakery fire. Before that some dodgy old gangster found his wife murdered in an odd way. Maybe three weeks ago, out on Long Island, Bob Shure found his mistress in a six foot block of tallow wax."

"Bob Shure, of Shure-Light Candles? Why would anyone want to kill his mistress?" Sandy asked, amazed.

"Who was the mobster?" Bob asked, as he got up to pour coffee.

"Vincent Sorrento," Ted said absently as he raised the steaming cup and inhaled deeply.

"Do you mean Vincent, the meat man? Sorrento's is a meat packing place that only sells to high end restaurants."

"What does it all mean?" Dave asked, trying to recount the nonsensical nature of the crime scenes.

"I don't know yet, but the Crimson Mask is going to find out," Bob said quietly, "Ted, I'll need anything you can get me on these murders. I'll be going back to every scene. Also get a list of any other less-than-regular crimes that have been reported since the first of the year."

"Dave, I'll need you to watch the store in my absence, and keep your eyes peeled for anything that is out of the ordinary in the news."

The rotund little fellow's cheeks flushed as he replied, "peeling one's eyes, thanks boss."

"Sandy, I'll need all the dirt you can dig up on the closest family members of the victims; these staged scenes are too odd to be random." He looked at them each in turn, "All of you be wary and watchful. When this guy, or guys, gets an earful that we're after them … Well, I don't want to find any of you hemmed up any of the ways I've had to deal with evil."

Ted grinned, "Yeah, neither do we."

The grim dead end of Stooksbury Road, the contrast between the freshness of the early spring morning and the somber mourning of the family was stark. The Crimson Mask stood stalwart against the chilling breeze, darkening the doorstep of Vincent Sorrento's eldest son. He knocked three times, hard.

Eventually sounds from within ended in heavy footfalls on creaking wooden floorboards. A tallish, fit, thirty-something man came to the door, his Neapolitan features barely contained his muscular visage. "Yeah'r, what is it?" he said as the door opened. When he realized he was looking into the chest of a larger, fitter man in a dark suit he looked upward into the fedora shadowed face, hidden by a domino mask, his jaw clenched.

"I'm the Crimson Mask. I'm looking for Vincent Sorrento," he said in a firm, commanding tone.

"I kna' who y'are, what'dya want with the old man?" The man's steely eyes tried to pierce the Mask's own gaze.

"What's your name, Sir?" The Mask asked him, answering his question with a question.

"Valentino Sorrento, what do you want with my father?"

"I'm sorry about your mother, I'm here to help. I need to speak with your father, and I need to take a look at the scene. I'm going to help the police put together a puzzle that starts with murder in Hell's Kitchen."

The fellow looked left, right, and up the block. "Come in. You're not too popular around here, for obvious reasons. Pop's out, he likes to go to the plant and talk to the young guys that work on the dock and in the meat room. I think it does him good; retirement will be hard on him."

"Plant?" the Mask asked, knowing that most people love to talk about themselves and their family accomplishments, especially immigrants.

"Yes, my father grew his father's neighborhood butcher shop into a packing house that supplies all the finest restaurants in all five boroughs in New York City with the finest quality meat."

"I'm aware of your father's involvement with a number of organized crime syndicates," the Crimson Mask ventured.

"Look pal, the old man got out of the rackets back in '25. When things the families started turned one on another, the old man retired. There's a lot about it he'll carry to his grave. I came up in the business, and any time I ran errands or collected numbers and he heard about it, he unleashed the strap on my back end. He was the only one of a dozen brothers who made it out."

"Many guys never get out. Why your father? What happened back in 1925 that sent your father here from the classy places over on Delaney?"

"It was nothing he was into, it was somethin' my brothers and I got into," the fellow seemed to deflate. "The money from booze was petering out. The plant was doing great, but me and Tommy and James got in our heads we were going to make our own way. You know, through the rackets. So we took an interest into the reefer business they run over in Harlem. We stole a truck load of it and sold it to get the money to buy a restaurant. People transacting business …" He shrugged. "Another murder joint. Meantime, those guys in Harlem found out who took their rope dope and put a hit out. Their consigliore came to see my old man. Out of respect. He knew Pop from the old days. The old man contracted with a guy in the Kitchen who cleans stuff up, to take care of it."

"An assassin?" The masked man asked, already knowing the truth.

The fellow nodded. "The guy they sent to kill us was a marked man. He was among other things a very bad thief. The cleaner had a very long memory, and instead of just doing the cleanup, he sent a message. He garroted the guy and then cut off his hands. He sent them to the guy's mother in a cookie jar."

"Do you think the rival operation in Harlem had something to do with your mother's murder?" The Mask asked Valentino, not entirely sure of it himself, but trying to gauge the man's proclivity for unilateral response.

The guy crossed his arms and his head sank to his chest for a moment as he exhaled deeply, "Y'know, I tried to talk to the old man about it. He's all broke up, in here," he gestured to his heart. "He don't think so, but he don't know what else to think. I wanted to send a guy to check it out. The boys are just dying to go to Harlem and start an all out war. The old man, he said no."

"Can I see the scene?" The part of the Crimson Mask that was compassionate wanted to reach out to the man, to comfort him, but the uncompromising crime fighter felt that finding the killer would be consolation enough.

"Yeah, let me get my coat."

"I hope you understand if I ask you to leave me to my work," The Mask said rather insistently when Valentino started into his father's apartment ahead of him.

"No, I don't mind. The old man hasn't spent a night in there since. He's talking about renting it out. I don't think he can stand being in there, after …"

"Has anyone else been in there?"

The man thought for a moment, "Other than the cops, and the old man's couple of trips in for things he needed, no."

"Can I see the scene?"

"Don't let him rent it until I tell you. The police may have released the scene, but I'm sure they missed something. They always miss something," the Crimson Mask said, as he entered the foyer and switched on the light.

"Yeah, cops got a nose for other people's business until it's time to go to work," Valentino quipped.

"That's a little disrespectful don't you think? None of the beat cops and less than a dozen detectives have any specialized training for what they do. They're mostly well intentioned men with very busy minds trying to unravel the evils of a very large piece of real estate," He chastened.

"Sorry, I didn't mean anything by it. Just sore when it hits home," Valentino said, receding a bit. Valentino turned to exit. "I'll leave you to your work," the Mask nodded, noting the pain on the man's face.

As the door closed behind him, the Crimson Mask recited the details of the crime scene report from memory. The distinct aroma of blood still hung in the stagnant air of the apartment. He walked through the kitchen, looking for anything out of place. There was nothing worthy of note except the empty space between the salt and pepper mills where he assumed the cookie jar had sat.

The dining room was undisturbed, though the roll top on the desk was up and the lap drawer was open slightly. He turned on the banker's lamp on the desk. He turned around and looked at the table. One chair was slightly ajar, the chair at the corner of the table nearest the doorway to the living room.

He drew open the drapes in the living room and turned on every light bulb. He surveyed the scene and oriented himself to the rug, so that he was standing near where the victim's feet would have been. Without even bending over, the Crimson Mask found his first clue.

He walked to the opposite end of the rug and knelt just above where the head of Graciela Sorrento would have pounded the rug as she gasped for air. He saw two distinctly different varieties of hair. There were greying black hairs stuck in the weave of the rug. He paid them no further attention after surmising that they were embedded in the weave of the braided rug.

The other hairs, of varying length and differing texture were something else, something else entirely. The red-brown hair was of a fine silky texture, though some were coarser. They varied from two to five inches in length. The Mask took an envelope from his breast pocket and placed several dozen of the hairs in it. He found similar hairs in the fascia of the pocket doors that separated the living room from the hallway.

After taking a piece of the blood soaked rug, and a bit of coiled wire that he found discarded near the baseboard, the Crimson Mask made his exit. He went next door to alert Valentino to his departure. When he knocked, it was the elder Sorrento who answered.

"It's you, the Crimson Mask. Valentino said you'd come." The old fellow looked wrung out.

"Yes sir, I'm finished. I need to take some samples to my lab. The police think that your wife's death might be connected to several other murders that have happened recently," the Mask said flatly.

The old man shot out a hand, catching the Crimson Mask by the arm,."You catch them. You catch them and punish them for what they've done. My Gracie never hurt a hair on anyone's head. No matter all my business, she had no part in none of it. She didn't deserve this."

"Mr. Sorrento, it is always the innocent who suffer the poor choices of others," the Crimson Mask sneered. "My work is to make criminals pay for their misdeeds."

The Crimson Mask watched from a distance as the procession stopped near the open gravesite in Portside Cemetery, Queens. He watched as the Bakers stepped out of the limousine and were escorted to the tent canopy where a dozen chairs were arranged next to a pedestal where six pall bearers had placed a wooden casket.

He quietly approached the line of cars from the far side and slipped into the limo the Bakers had arrived in. At the end of the funeral service, the grieving couple left the graveside and returned to the long black car. As the driver pulled away from the curb, the Crimson Mask turned to them and said, "Mr. Alvin Baker?"

"Yes, I'm Al Baker. Who are you and how'd you get in here?"

"Mr. Baker, the Queensborough Police have made repeated attempts to discuss your son's untimely death with you. They have arrived at the conclusion that he may have been targeted because of your business dealings. I've come to offer you a singular opportunity to cooperate with my investigation."

Baker tried to glower, "I already talked to that detective, a Sergeant Somebody, and that kid what just got promoted, it was in the papers."

"Yes, and both of them came to the same conclusion. They both believe that you're hiding something. I can tell even now that this subject is far more uncomfortable for you than the funeral of your son. You're displaying an instinct of self preservation. Mr. Baker, you stink of fear."

"Alvin, what is he talking about?" Mrs. Baker asked in a very insistent wifely tone, calculated for distance and penetration.

The Crimson Mask took note that while both displayed the outward signs of funerary grief, neither of them were particularly distraught. Neither of them seemed like the common neighborhood baker. Their demeanor was outwardly unfriendly, coarse to him, defensive. Not people who were trying to make it by selling to regular customers and trying to earn new ones. These people were hiding something, and the wife wasn't happy about it.

"I'll be at the store tomorrow morning early. We're supposed to reopen. You want to talk to me, be there at six," Alvin hissed, after that he turned away from the Mask and after a quiet exchange with his wife, he leaned forward, "Hey, driver. This isn't the way to the funeral home, and we don't live down here."

Sandra Gray, dressed in a black suit and driving cap, looked up at the rearview mirror catching a nod from the Crimson Mask. "Sit back, Mr. Baker, this won't take long." She stomped the accelerator and made for 59th Street.

Baker turned on the Mask and once again tried to assert himself, "What's it with you people? I told ya when I'd meet with you."

"I told you I would offer you this one opportunity. I didn't ask you to check your schedule. I know you have nothing else planned for today. You are grieving, after all." Baker was silenced by the implied allegations and sat back against the seat. He didn't notice his wife shift her body slightly away from him, but the Crimson Mask noticed.

Fifteen minutes later Sandra turned on to Garrison Avenue off 59th Street and stopped thirty feet from the corner, pulling up in front of Baker's Bakery. The Crimson Mask opened the door and got out of the car. The Bakers paused as if waiting for something, Mr. Baker going so far as clearing his throat to gain Sandra's attention.

"If I were potentially being ruled a suspect in a conspiracy related to my son's murder, I think I'd take the initiative of opening my own doors," she said as she glared at him in the mirror.

Mrs. Baker likewise glared at Alvin and pulled the lever, opening her door and stepping out of the car. When he attempted to follow her, she quickly slammed the car door. He in turn opened the door and was threatening Sandra with a call to the funeral director when she stepped on the gas and drove away.

"Alvin, I think it might be a good time for you to knock off acting like a horse's ass and start cooperating," Mrs. Baker growled at him as they made their way to the front door, where the Crimson Mask waited with forced patience. Mrs. Baker was doing the hard part so far while he simply provided the approval for her to say what was on her mind.

Alvin produced a key and unlocked the door. As they entered he walked behind the counter and switched on the lights. Mrs. Baker locked the door behind them and didn't turn the closed sign. She approached the counter, standing near the Crimson Mask, who was watching Alvin's reaction to his presence in the bakery. Alvin simply rocked on his heels.

"Mrs. Baker, would you make some coffee? Mr. Baker is going to show me around. It may take us a while," he said with an edge in his voice, something she couldn't quite place, but Alvin got loud and clear.

"But I have accounts that need reconciling. We need to get this place cleaned up before we reopen tomorrow. I have too much to get done, I can't just sit idle," Alvin said, making an attempt to excuse himself from further scrutiny.

"Then we should get to it," the Mask said as he walked behind the counter toward the kitchen.

In the basement kitchen, the scene was largely as the police had left it. Flour on the floor bore a number of foot prints. Areas of higher traffic bore many sets of tracks making it quite difficult to distinguish one set from another. Alvin started to enter the kitchen, but the Crimson Mask stopped him. "Mr. Baker, I have to ask you to stop here and let me do my work."

Baker gave him a look, but stepped away from the doorway. The Mask first assessed the scene from the doorway. He saw a number of things in his initial look that caused him some concern. From memory again he went through the crime scene report and then through his mental checklist. He liked to observe the scene from floor to ceiling and immediately something didn't feel right.

"Mr. Baker, tell me what the police had to say, from the minute the phone rang until your last conversation with Sergeant York that motivated you to begin avoiding the police."

"I don't like your accusations, Mr. Mask. What are you hiding that you need to wear a mask and pull your hat down over your eyes?"

"So you persist in avoiding questioning, even at the expense of bringing your son's killer to justice."

Baker pulled up short, "Well no, but I don't like being accused of having anything to do with it."

"You have used the word accused twice, though I have not accused you of anything. This is the sign of a guilty conscience weighing on a mind heavy with shame. If you have nothing to be ashamed of, why are you not more willing to assist me in bringing a killer to justice? Even your wife knows that you are hiding something. Tragic events generally push people together, especially the parents of a dead child. This is plainly pulling you apart. So you can either tell me, or I can ask her, and she will tell me, if she knows."

Baker started to speak and then paused. "The police, and the fire marshal all said that at first hand it looks like a dust explosion. There's smoke damage around the tops of the walls, I looked around and didn't argue. I was in shock, but something about it was familiar. Like the way the work tables had been moved around."

The Crimson Mask fished an envelope from his breast pocket and began collecting red brown hairs from the exterior doorjamb. He surmised that the killer had leaned against the doorway and observed his victim for several moments before he sprang into action.

"How were the tables moved around? How had they been arranged previously?" He asked in forceful, rapid fire.

"They were central down the length, in front of the ovens!" Baker exclaimed. "But somebody arranged them like ..." Baker trailed off.

The Crimson Mask's gaze was fixed on the scene, and it was as if he were balancing on the sound of Alvin Baker's voice. When the man stopped speaking he momentarily broke his scanning of the scene to look into the man's beady eyes.

"Like what, Baker? What familiarity is cause for your pregnant pause? Tell me, what ironic evil from your past has walked over your grave en route to déja`vu?" The Mask asked him with that keen edge in his voice. His gaze piercing, his eyes aflame from beneath the brim of his fedora, a terrifying glare from behind the shimmering velvet of the blood colored domino mask.

Baker's resolve broke under the Mask's penetrating gaze. His cheeks flushed and he began to sweat profusely. He was in the Crimson Mask's power, and they both knew that it was a pointless act to resist.

"Tell me now what this scene reminds you of. What did you do that has caused this evil to befall your family?" His voice was like a high carbon blade being drawn across a whetstone.

Baker spoke quickly, "Back in '29 when it all collapsed, my building and loan folded on the day of the bank run. I took all the client funds and torched my office. I filed a claim but the insurance company was bust."

The Mask lunged, lightning quick he glowered over Baker, causing him to cower low. "Money? You expect me to believe that someone went to all this trouble for money? Tell me the truth, Baker, there's a special place in hell for people who cheat the boatman."

"My clerk, Mitch Curry, he lived in a shotgun house just a couple of blocks from the office. When he heard the fire brigade he went to check on our office. He went in before the fire truck got there and he didn't make it out. The tables are arranged in the basic shape of our office arrangement."

"He died trying to put out the fire of your greed?" the Mask growled in disgust.

Baker began to weep, "His body was found in front of the open safe. I never said a word."

"You're good at that, letting others stand in your place when judgment is coming. You say you never mentioned anything out of place when the police summoned you. Was it an open casket funeral?" Baker nodded vigorously. "Tell me, Baker, if this was a dust explosion how is it that your son was not burned?"

Baker was wide eyed, "I don't know. I hadn't been in the store all day. The wife and I had business in Brooklyn. When we were done we went home. You gotta find the guy who done this. The boy was my wife's reason for life. I could carve my own liver and it wouldn't faze her, but she'd face down a New York Central Hudson for the kid. She would have left when the firm failed, fine by me but she'd have taken my son. He was just like her, only wanted more and better but not willing to work for it. This is the first time she's been in here since the day I opened this place up again. The boy would never have made it at the office, but he had a talent for this. I wanted to leave it for him. He was my boy, now he's gone. You gotta turn me in for the other thing, that's fine. But get the guy who killed our boy."

The Crimson Mask entered the crime scene. The flour crunched like snow under his feet. Something about it felt wrong. None of the flour on the floor was charred. One table askew to the left was piled with tools and equipment. The other table, askew to the right was bare and had been wiped clean. Something in the way the light glimmered on the surface of the table caught his eye, but as he walked toward it he stopped short.

On the floor in the flour dust was the outline where the body had laid. The boy had made a scrambling fall. Sliding impressions were long and wide. "He was being attacked." The Crimson Mask followed the sliding track from just inside the kitchen door to the place where the body had come to its final rest. As if conducting an orchestra he followed the choreography of the attack in his mind's eye. As he lowered his hands, and his gaze to the resting place he saw them, what he'd first dismissed as the pivots of the boy's feet.

A completely different set of prints—belonging to someone who was very agile, but carried his weight far forward on the balls of his feet—were tactically placed. Whoever the murderer was, he was as aggressive as he was graceful.

The Mask produced a tongue depressor and a small canister. Carefully he took a sample of a blackish gummy mass which was matted with short hair of a flaxen color and texture. As he stood up, he saw the place where a wooden truncheon had laid in the flour. "What business would a juggler's pin have in a bakery?"

A short distance beyond the second table a kraft paper flour sack was on the floor. He walked over to it, giving a wide berth to the area where the body had laid. The bag was ruptured in several places as if it had been struck with great force. When he tried to pick it up, the bag suddenly tore and ten pounds of flour fell to the floor and then rose in a roiling cloud of smoke-like dust.

The Crimson Mask covered his mouth and nose with one hand and shook out his handkerchief with the other. He held the makeshift filter over his mouth and nose and made for the door. As he passed by the near table, the one that had been wiped, a thunderous sneeze erupted simultaneously from his upper and lower sinus as the gluten in the flour agitated his gag reflex.

The sneeze tore out of his head and blew most of the settling dust off the table, leaving behind only what had stuck to the residue on the tabletop. As the Crimson Mask opened his eyes he glared at the scrawled writing that had appeared. The simple message read: Rub-a-dub-dub.

Just after dark Bob Clarke arrived at his drug store. He entered and locked the door behind him. The store had been closed a mere half hour and the air still hung with the presence of Dave Small. Clarke made directly for the back room that served as the Crimson Mask's secret lab. On a lab table he laid out the evidence from the two scenes he'd visited. The eerie message from the bakery rolled around his mind like a marble in a track.

The things that were similar in nature were the red brown hairs, of varied texture and length, suggesting hair from different parts of the body;

head, chest, arm, etc. The wire from the first scene was unique in some way. He was sure it was a piece of the garrote that had been used to kill Mrs. Sorrento. There was the blood soaked rug and the mass of hair and blood cemented with what was most likely whole wheat flour.

He took two small cards. On one he drew the truncheon and laid it with the evidence from the bakery; on the other he wrote 'Rub-a-dub-dub' and placed it with the evidence from the bakery as well. Then he remembered the cookie jar Valentino had told him about. He wrote, 'Rub-a-dub-dub?' on a third card and placed it with the Stooksbury Road evidence.

He set the percolator over the Bunsen burner again and paced while the coffee brewed. "Butcher is simple, Sorrento was a butcher. Baker was a baker, so that was also simple. He hadn't been to the tallow works as yet, but he agreed with Sandy. Why would someone kill the mistress of a man that everyone knew to be a kindly and upstanding guy? Bob Shure had been a renowned bachelor. He had no children and had only been seen around with one woman." He continued pacing the length of the room until the coffee was done.

He filled his cup with the oily black liquid and stirred in a tablespoonful of sorghum molasses. He sat at the side table and opened a ledger in which he'd started collecting his thoughts on the various cases, first from the police reports, and now from his own investigations at the crime scenes. He had started a page for each case and left the following page spread blank so that, just as an accountant might flow the columns from page to page by account, he would have the option of doing so as well, identifying a column in each spreadsheet for the other cases so that evidence of a similar nature could be recorded in an organized fashion and save a lot of page turning for simple detail.

He rested his head on his hand while recording an hypothesis on a sheet from a stenographer's notebook. His eyes were growing heavy, but he had more to get done. Bob poured his third cup of coffee and added the molasses. He sat down at the table and picked up his pen.

"How can you drink that?" Dave Small exclaimed, not having found the boss asleep in the lab for a while.

Doc Clarke's eye's shot open and he stretched reflexively, "Time?"

"Five-thirty," Dave said quietly as he moved the jar of molasses away from the percolator and started cleaning the lab, coffee maker first.

"Aren't you early?" Doc Clarke asked, as he stood up and continued to stretch.

"You're not going to be around much, so I thought I'd come in early and get the weekly cleaning done. We're always slow on Wednesdays," he said absently as he dumped a measure of beans into the coffee grinder.

"Careful. I used that to powder some zinc for Martha Daniel's cold remedy," Bob said as he slipped on his coat.

"What was in it?" Dave said, pausing only long enough to get the question out.

"Zinc, ascorbic acid, capsicum, willow bark, and Echinacea," Doc Clarke recited from memory.

"How'd she say it worked?" Dave asked as he continued to grind.

"She said it took about a week to work. There's more there in the commode table next to the pharmadex."

"Zinc, vitamin c, cayenne pepper, aspirin, and ma nature's cure all. Let's give it a go, shall we?" Dave said as he added a teaspoon of the mixture to the coffee grounds.

"Be careful with that, you might not have a sniffle for two years," Bob said as he went for the door. "I'm going home to get cleaned up. The Crimson Mask is visiting a candle factory and the theater and if I'm going to be around all those actresses I can't look like I slept in a dust bin."

"I'll mind the store and get as much of the weekly business tidied up as I can. I have to be at the Hospital tomorrow, so I won't be around until later," Dave said as Doc Clarke was making his exit.

Ted Warrick sat at the dining room table with a small wooden chest in front of him. He poured three fingers worth of scotch into a glass and took a long draw on it. He refilled the glass and released the latch on the chest. He opened the lid and paused a moment to clasp his hands and say a quiet prayer.

He lifted a framed photograph from the chest. He looked into the eyes of the taller of the two patrolmen. "I have done my best to do right by you, and by him," he said as he set the photograph aside.

The next item he lifted from the chest was an old .32 caliber police special revolver. He depressed the lever and swung the barrel down. He gave the empty cylinder a spin and unsnapped the ammo pouch attached to the holster. He inserted both three round half-moon clips into the cylinder and closed the action. He slipped the six inch revolver back into its cross-draw holster and closed the flap.

He set out a small porcelain tin containing a badge and a number of medals. He set aside his framed letter of appointment as Police

"I have done my best to do right by you, and by him."

Commissioner. A small wooden tray held three small black books, his beat books, where he'd made notes on citizen contacts while walking a foot beat. He picked up a small brown glass jar, the size of a pill bottle. He gave it a shake and sixteen single ought buckshot pellets and a .45/70 slug rattled inside.

Warrick had been thinking about the bizarre nature of the murders, and what Bob Clarke had said in jest. He knew enough about Sandra and Dave Small to know that they had relatively nothing to fear from this killer who seemed to have a personal vendetta against anyone who used or caused misfortune to others for personal gain.

Though he'd retired as Commissioner, Ted had been a beat cop. He'd blown the whistle on cops and turned his head on petty criminals, and vice versa. He realized the value of the grey area between the letter of the law and its formal function. He made the focus of his police work to bring real criminals to justice and not criminalize people who were having a hard time providing for their families. But there had been more than a few questionable situations. One of which had haunted him for years.

He lifted a brown record jacket out of the bottom of the chest and placed it alongside the holstered pistol. After returning the other items to the chest Ted closed the lid and fastened the latch. He placed the chest on the mantelpiece where it had sat these many years. He tucked the revolver into the pocket of his smoking jacket and cradled the file under his arm. He drained the glass of scotch and carried it and the bottle to the desk in the corner of the alcove that served at his study.

A night of haunted slumber was his only reward for searching the files with officer Whiskey. The official report and the eyewitness account of Sergeant Clarke's murder had been reported as gangster activity. But he'd heard, and seen, and theorized an alternate chain of events orchestrated by someone moving within the dark side of the city's shadow. A dozen accounts in as many years of bad men dying bizarre and horrific deaths. He'd discounted all of them save one; the one that had sent the promising intellect of his best friend's only child on its quest to make criminals pay for their misdeeds.

In his final nightmare of what had been a tragic night of alcohol induced slumber, Ted Warrick relived the night of his best friend's death as the figure eight cycle of a very long day. A spatter of horrific memory, details of a thousand different cases, and untinctured guilt swirled together to set every scene with the common theatrical devices of that night.

No matter if it were in a basement, a warehouse, the docks, or a rooftop it was always the body of his friend. Always a boy standing over the death-masked corpse of his father, always crying out in tortured grief, and that boy's gaze always looked up from his father's empty eyes wearing a crimson domino mask.

Ted didn't know what any of it meant, other than whoever had committed the early murders was evidently back in business. The last one had been the murder of Bob's father. The others had been swept under the rug in the mad dash to catch gangsters who killed a cop. But it had never satisfied him. He was still puzzling on it when he went to the door to get the morning paper.

Ted opened the front door just as Bob Clarke was raising a fist to knock. "Oh!"

"Expecting me?" Bob asked, a smile cracking the corner of his mouth.

"No, not really. Quite the opposite, in fact," he said over his shoulder as Ted entered and closed the door behind him, turning the bolt.

Bob knew something was up when Ted went to the study and sat down, putting the large cherry desk between them. He knew it was something bad when he saw the open file and the holstered revolver. He took the glass and the empty bottle of scotch away and returned to the small study with a pitcher of water and glass. "Do you want to talk about it? Or will you even if you don't want to?" He asked as he fished in an inside pocket of his coat.

Ted ran a hand over his face, "I'd rather not actually, but I am almost certain that we need to have this discussion. I fear that my life may depend on it."

Bob, a bit perturbed by Ted's abnormal demeanor and the assertion that he was in danger, selected a folded paper pouch from a leather clutch and returned it to his coat. The envelope contained a powder which he emptied into the glass before filling it with water. He pushed it across the desk.

"What's this?" Ted asked, eyeing the fizzling glass with some curiosity and suspicion.

"Something to ward off the dog that bit you," Bob said as he sat down.

Ted raised an eyebrow and reached for the glass. He gave Doc Clarke another look.

"Ted, it's a headache compound I am testing. Sodium Bicarbonate, aspirin, aluminum salts, and an anti-peptide, it should alleviate your headache, cause you to retain fluids and settle your stomach," Bob explained.

Ted downed the liquid and held out the glass which Bob refilled. He took several long sips and sat the glass on the desk.

"Now tell me what's got you in the bottle?" Bob said with an insistent edge in his voice.

Ted regarded him for a long moment and inhaled deeply before a long exhale pushed through his pained expression. "What you have to understand is that this has just occurred to me suddenly, that these cases are of a similar nature to a dozen bizarre killings that happened in the years leading up to your father's murder. I don't know if they were related, or connected at all, but I remember wondering very seriously at the time and now if there was some such connection, and how it might have involved either your father or me."

Bob sat for a moment just listening and let it sink in. "Go on. What are you trying to tell me? Surely not that you had anything to do with my father being killed. That's ridiculous."

Ted shook his head, "It is and it isn't. You know very well that the criminal mind is different from the mind of the average man. Different in its reasoning of right, wrong, and appropriate response to perceived wrong."

"These other murders, were they done as elaborate set pieces? Or were they odd in their cause and manner?" Bob asked rather insistently.

"It wasn't odd in cause and manner, but a dead man placed at a piano in a store window, pushed in front of a train, all kinds of strange circumstance. But never close, it was one a year or two in a year and it skipped a couple years. I will see what I can dig up in records, but you know they only hold on to stuff so long," Ted explained further, "It was always very precise, though. Bullets struck with such precision that a long range marksman was called in to tell us how they were doing it. Stabbings also very surgical in nature, cuts made with light, very sharp knives, but none of the tools were ever left. I can't say for sure that any of them are linked, or even if the same men are responsible, but when the bullet left Tom with that mark, I could only assume."

Bob stood up. "Any information you can get for me will no doubt be beneficial. The recent cases are almost definitely linked. I've found the same hair and a bizarre situation at two scenes. Today the Crimson Mask will return to the Cohan Theater and head out to Long Island to Shure Light to see the woman encased in tallow wax. You may come along if you like."

"Give me an hour to get ready," Ted said, draining the last of his water glass, "and bring along a couple of those headache powders."

Bob Clarke left the Warrick residence with a full and busy mind. He returned to the drug store to collect a toolbox into which he'd gathered some items essential to his investigations, not the least of which was a bifocal magnifying glass.

Broadway, later that morning, the Crimson Mask's roadster angled in at the curb in front of the Cohan Theater. He and Warrick entered the theater and crossed the grand lobby. They were met by none other than George M. Cohan himself on their way to the main theater office. After a brief exchange and an open ended invitation to the next production, Cohan passed them off to a maintenance man with his blessing to comb Astrid Minx's dressing room for evidence.

The dressing room door still bore the gold star and the plaque stating Astrid E. Minx, but the interior was totally empty with the exception of the folding chair, field desk and area around the crime scene. The floor had not been swept, and the counters and mirror had not been cleaned, but all of Ms. Minx's things had been removed.

"This one doesn't figure," the Crimson Mask said to Ted as he scanned the scene.

"What about it doesn't figure? The victim, Tom O'Donnell, was murdered while his gal was singing her heart out. He had his throat cut and the bottle stuck in his back," Ted countered.

"Well, the coroner confirmed what I would have surmised, that the exsanguination was caused by the severing of the carotid artery, not the multiple superficial and single subcutaneous punctures to the back almost directly over the scapula," the Crimson Mask explained.

"No major blood vessels. So why bother?" Ted replied as he gestured to the map of the OH-PENN Natural Gas range that was heavily obscured by the late Tom O'Donnell's dried blood. "And why kill him here? I'm sure Astrid Minx has never wronged anyone sufficiently to provoke homicidal retribution."

The Mask finished collecting his samples and started to fasten the lids on the small jars when he replied. "I don't think this had anything to do with Astrid Minx, and I doubt it was anything to do with Cohan, or even Tom O'Donnell who has a reputation as a bit of a spoiled would-be hoodlum. I need to talk to Astrid."

They left the dressing room and walked into an argument between the stage manager and choreographer about some petty internal matter. Warrick, content to wait patiently for a cease fire paused momentarily.

The Crimson Mask, on the case, inserted himself between them and demanded, "Tell me where I can find Astrid Minx."

Neither of them spoke, both of them eyed him coolly. The choreographer tried to move in one direction and the stage manager in the other, but he caught them both. "I asked you where I could find Astrid Minx."

"We're between productions, all of the talent and especially the ones with corpses in their dressing rooms are laid off," the stage manager snipped.

Lindenhurst, Long Island, that afternoon. Ted Warrick was in awe as he and the Crimson Mask stood before the six foot block of paraffin-tallowate. Neither he nor the Crimson Mask knew exactly what to say to the obviously grieving Bob Shure, whose longtime mistress had been cast in wax like a fly caught in amber.

"I'm still in complete shock that anyone would want to kill Janine. She was a very giving woman. It was among the things that I loved most about her. She was beautiful and kind. She was gentle," Shure said quietly.

"Did you have a business or personal dealing with anyone at any time that may have gone bad? Did you ever take advantage of having the upper hand with an employee, or did you ever have relations with a married woman who had a jealous spouse?" the Crimson Mask asked as he thrust a few red brown hairs into an envelope.

Shure looked thoughtful but ultimately shook his head. "No. I haven't had trouble with another person for a long time. Janine went through a really bad divorce. She was pregnant and lost the baby. Her husband beat her bad. He was a real bad seed. We hadn't known each other long, and he got wind of it and threatened her. She was afraid because she knew the stuff he'd done."

The Crimson Mask sharp eyes focused on Shure, "Where is he? Is he still in town?"

Shure shook his head. "We heard he'd gone out west somewhere. Somebody said they saw him down south. I don't know anything more than he was in the pen and we heard he was out."

"So you and Janine were married after her divorce?" Ted asked abrasively.

Shure shook his head. "No. I don't know why we didn't. It just didn't seem important. She was safe when he went away and never brought up marriage."

They were heading out and the Crimson Mask turned and asked Bob Shure one last question as he excused himself. "Was it your baby she lost?" Bob Shure's broken expression told him all he needed to know.

Bob Clarke was filling a prescription for Coke syrup when the red light beneath the rear counter began to pulse slowly. There were two customers waiting: One for the syrup he had prepared; the other, Mister Sparks, was waiting for a bottle of strong ammonia and a bottle of iodine crystals. He picked up the receiver to the special phone line, "Yes?"

The voice of Ted Warrick said, "I just received two calls, one from Sergeant Paul Garret asking if I'd heard about any strange writings at any of the scenes. He didn't say why at first, but it seems that when the maid cleaned Astrid Minx's dressing room the words, 'Three men in a tub,' appeared when she rubbed a vinegar soaked newspaper across the mirror."

"One moment, sir, I have a customer," Doc Clarke said and set down the handset. He slipped the small bottle of syrup into a brown bag and went to the front counter. He handed the package to Mrs. Tillman and dropped her fifty cents in the till.

"Mr. Sparks, your Iodine." He drew a small glass vial out of a drawer, "and a quart of strong ammonia." He took a quart sized brown glass bottle down from a high shelf and sat it alongside the vial of iodine crystals. "That will be three dollars." The older fellow handed him a silver dollar and a two dollar bill. Doc Clarke took his money and smiled. "Mr. Sparks, what are you doing with iodine and ammonia?"

Sparks smiled. "Fulminate." He grinned broadly. "I'm trying to build a better mousetrap." The two shared a smile and Bob went back to the phone as the old fellow made his exit. "Okay Ted, go ahead."

"Oh, err, yes. Garret was asking about strange writings after the mirror, and then Carl York rang me from the five-nine. He wanted to know if there was anything like it at the Hell's Kitchen scene."

"I didn't see anything of the sort at Stooksbury Road. I wasn't looking; maybe it was there and I didn't find it. I need to go back and look. The same for Shure Light; I didn't notice it, but I think Bob Shure was hiding something. I'll pay him a surprise visit tonight. The Crimson Mask will be in the neighborhood."

"The police are getting antsy, wondering if their next call or the next thing they walk up on is going to be one of these bizarre killings," Ted said in his fatherly watch commander's tone.

"I got it, but I'm afraid that until things break loose all we can do is wait," Bob said in frustration.

"Do you plan to wait? Surely you don't think you'll just happen to catch them in the act?" Ted said in exasperation.

"On the contrary, alert the precincts that until this breaks I need to be called to every murder scene as soon as they're discovered."

"Okay, will do. Will there be anything else?" Ted asked.

"Yes, do you save newspapers?"

"Yes I do. Why?"

"Go through them looking for every shady business deal, every jealous husband, and every schoolyard bully. When you pick up a pattern starting with the earliest case you can get police reports to substantiate. Explain to Garret and York what you are doing and get one reliable sergeant from the other boroughs to do the same. Keep it quiet. Precincts are like sponges, lots of little holes. Rats live in little holes. Meet with all of them someplace quiet and get back to me as soon as you find anything. Remember, this is classified, need to know only, and get the kind of guys who can be trusted. If they aren't worth taking a bullet for, they're the wrong ones," Clarke said quickly and hung up the phone.

Sandra was driving through Alder Brook, the neighborhood that terminated just east of five points. She slowed to wait on some traffic obstruction in front of Beryl's, a green grocer who had the best sweet corn in Manhattan. As she waited a carnival wagon passed. Acrobats, clowns, and a marching band made their way along the high street, but the thing that most drew her attention was the colorful signage for the freak show.

She felt a surge of sorrow and curiosity as a buckboard carrying the bearded lady and the man ape passed, drawn by the strongman, who labored at the yoke like a draft animal. She mulled it as the last wagon rolled into the distance and traffic started to move again. She stopped at the corner, and as she waited to turn, Sandra glanced left and read the sign on the back of the last wagon: *Thrills and Chills Await at the Coney Island Carnival.*

She thought of the thick hair covering the man ape, and the sad, terrified eyes of the bearded lady. She pursed her lips and swallowed hard at the mental image of the man pulling the buckboard, the way he stared at the street and didn't look up at the people who gawked at him.

"It must be hard to be different. Being paraded through the streets everywhere you go just adds insult to injury," she said absently as she made the turn and started to speed away. Suddenly her eyes flashed at the rearview mirror and lit on the now unreadable sign on the back of the wagon. "That's it!" She turned the roadster around on a dime and sped back toward lower Manhattan.

Ted Warrick walked into the smoke filled barroom and approached the mahogany slab. The quiet man behind the bar raised his chin from the glass he was drying just enough to notice Ted knock once and tap with his index finger. He nodded slightly and shelved the Collins glass before drawing a beer into a pilsner and pouring a dram of Irish whiskey.

An old fellow shrouded in the shadow at the end of the bar took notice of Ted and swirled the last of the dark red wine in his glass. He tipped it high and set the empty vessel on the bar. He gestured the sign of the cross and said, "Salut." He slipped off the stool and went to the high-back next to Ted.

"You're Warrick. I know you from the old days," the man said respectfully.

"And you are Vincenza Sorrento. I know you, also from the old days," Ted said with a slightly reverent smile.

"What brings you down to Hell's Kitchen?" Sorrento asked with a tinge of the old edge in his voice.

"I'm here on business," Ted said quietly, taking a sip of the dram.

"Jack doesn't allow business in here, he runs a clean joint. When Frankie got it, the kid swore off family business. He took his inheritance and opened this joint, the first night he called the cops on two guys counting the take from their racket."

"That's why I'm here. I need to meet with some people on neutral ground where the walls don't hear so much."

The barkeep brought another glass of wine to Sorrento and said, "You come to the right place."

Within the hour they started arriving. First Carl York arrived via taxi. Minutes later as he and Ted were settling into the private dining room, Paul Garret entered. Bill Schroeder, the Detective Sergeant from Brooklyn. The sergeants from The Bronx and Staten Island came in together, twins by the name of Edward and Phillip Washa.

A boy of about twelve years old entered with a serving card. He set a tray of cups and a pot of coffee in the center of the table. A few minutes later Jack Fratelli himself entered with the boy. "Gentlemen, welcome to Aces. If there's anything we can get for you while you're here, just say the word. This is my son, Francis. I wanted him to meet some guys who were holding up the law, not trying to crawl under it."

The men smiled at the connotation, and the Washa brothers shared in the good-natured discourse. "Thank you, Mr. Fratelli. Right now we're going to have our meeting, maybe drinks later."

Francis exited, and the elder Fratelli pulled the doors to the private dining room closed behind him. Ted Warrick started by pouring coffee for everyone. Everyone settled momentarily and Ted returned to his chair. After a few minutes of quiet reflection he sat up and said, "Are there any questions before we get into this?"

It was Bill Schroeder who spoke up. "Well, Warrick, not for nothin', but I don't think I'm alone in wondering what retired commissioner has a random get up with a bunch of nobody's from the boroughs, in a former bootleg joint?"

A week later, Dave Small was demonstrating a chemical process for Doc Clarke. It was after 10:00 p.m. and the store was closed. The scent of ammonia was thick in the air and both Doc and Dave were wearing filter cones over their mouths and noses.

"A better mousetrap you say?" Dave said across the table as Doc looked on.

"Yes, and he said it with a straight face," Doc Clarke said with a curious twinkle in his eye.

"I don't know about mice, but it would make a pretty fair woman repellant," Dave said shaking his head at the intense stench that rose as he swirled in the iodine crystals.

Within a minute of reaching its critical temperature the ammonia began to reduce and crystals started to reform. When the crystalline structures started to stick to the glass rod he used for stirring, Dave removed the rod and grasped the beaker with his leather gloved hand. Round and round he slowly swirled as the crystals rolled in the rapidly evaporating liquid.

As the first crystals began to rattle against the sides, having depleted nearly all of the liquid, Dave removed the beaker from the heat and gently poured the crystals and the few drops of solution onto thick fibrous paper. "They should be stable until completely cool and dry," he said quietly as he spread them around with the glass rod.

The door buzzer Doc Clarke had wired into the special phone line that connected retired Police Commissioner Ted Warrick to the Crimson Mask's secret lab began its ticking tirade. The doc began to step away when the glass rod slipped from Dave's fingers and fell end over end as if in slow motion. A frightened smile broke on Dave's face as he met Doc Clarke's gaze.

Doc lunged, knocking Dave off his feet and covering him with his own body as the ammonium tri-iodide crystals that had stuck to the glass rod were crushed between the rod and the floor. *PLAKKOW!* The fulminate detonated, shattering the glass rod into a fine, razor-sharp powder, leaving only a purple-brown stain around the point of impact.

"Whew!" Doc Clarke said as he got to his feet and waved away a curl of purplish smoke.

Dave sat up a bit dazed, "I think it's ready."

Just then the buzzer began its ticking again and Doc Clarke picked up the handset. "Clarke here."

"Bob, its Ted Warrick. I have a lead for you. I followed your direction and invited one trustworthy man from the main precinct in each borough. We met on neutral ground and agreed to begin sharing information between the six of us. As secure telephone lines are not practical, if we don't meet in person we will communicate via coded message. Those messages will be handled through the private post to boxes in each borough in the name of Otto Ottendorf."

"Excellent! What does Ottendorf like to read?" Clarke asked quietly.

"Crime and Punishment," Warrick replied.

"Dostoyevsky, brilliant. You mentioned a lead?" Bob asked a business edge evident in his voice.

"Yes, just now I received a message from The Bronx. Tonight around 8:30 p.m., a horse patrolman stopped to rest his mount. They were in Bronx Park, on Cornwallis Trail, about three quarters of a mile from the south entrance to the Bronx Zoo. Something spooked the horse. The patrolman said the thing was huge, man sized, covered with long hair. The horse reared and it was all he could do to stay on. Later he rode back through the area and found what he believed initially to be a hobo camp, but in the moonlight turned out to be a murder hole. We are meeting there at eleven-thirty; the Chief has ordered in trucks with aircraft lights."

"Don't let them in the scene until the Crimson Mask gets there," Doc said as he hung up the phone.

"Doc lunged, knocking Dave off his feet ..."

Within the hour the Crimson Mask was driving along the cobblestone surface of Cornwallis Trail in Bronx Park. He knew the scene by the army trucks with aircraft spotlights that were bathing a small depressed clearing at the edge of the tree line that followed the Bronx River. He parked the roadster behind a panel truck from Washa's smoked meats.

The Mask brought his scene kit and approached a big man wearing overalls. "Is Ted Warrick around here anywhere?"

The big man wheeled on him, staring down with piercing eyes. "So you're the Crimson Mask?"

"Yes. I need to speak with Warrick and then I need to get into the scene. I'm putting together bits and pieces of these cases, but the fresher the evidence, the better."

An icy smile curled the corners of the big man's marble jaw. "I'm Billy Schroeder. Warrick's probably in the truck with the twins. York and Garret are following a trail."

"Nice bacon truck," the Mask quipped.

"Can you think of a less obvious way for a bunch of cops to get around?" The big man laughed.

One of the rear doors of the truck was slightly ajar and when he reached for the lever, Ted Warrick pushed it open and stepped down. Introductions were made and the Crimson Mask headed for the local scene.

A tiny elongated clearing opened off the edge of Cornwallis Trail. At the far end the ground fell away into a knee-deep depression about twenty feet in diameter. In that low place, where the shadows played with the mind and the blood glistened black, four dead men were perched like hobos around a small fire.

From his box of crime scene tools, the Crimson Mask produced a carbide lamp which he turned on and clamped to a low branch to light the immediate area. He scanned the scene for evidence, but the flames and competing shadows and light sources made it nearly impossible. He eventually returned to the trucks and asked the driver of one of the military trucks to back into the clearing and turn the aircraft spotlight so that it lit the depression.

When the truck was in place and the light adjusted, the depression was bathed in a bright incandescent light. The scene was almost comic in its tragedy. Four obvious transients whose hard luck had finally turned to stone were staged in such pathetic order that even the most callous of the men were taken aback and shed real tears.

All of them had been killed, apparently with the same or similar long thin-bladed knife with a wickedly sharp edge. The two who appeared to be younger than the others bore defensive and offensive wounds. They had obviously tried to defend themselves and the others and paid with their lives.

Before the Crimson Mask allowed the scene to be raked clean of the minimal amount of evidence, he surveyed it from all angles and came to the conclusion that one man had been stirring a soup pot that contained water and an old shoe while another cradled a doll with a broken face, while the third and fourth were engaged in a sadistic scene with a pick and shovel. It was an absurd statement on the country's depression. These men's only apparent crime was being poor and on the move.

As the men were placed in more dignified positions for their imminent transport to Potter's Field, each was searched for any clue to why they might have been targeted, either as an individual or the group as a whole. The four collectively had twenty cents between them. Each man had a nickel in the right front pocket of his trousers with a note on a piece of folded paper which read:

Rub-a-dub-dub
Three men in a tub
Who might they be?
A Butcher
A Baker
A Candlestick maker
Men with dirty souls all three
Dead with a note they rode in a boat
Bound for the Carnival you see.

As they were finishing, Garret and York returned. Their hunt was not completely without merit, though they never caught sight of the beast which the patrolman had originally reported, nor the suspect who'd made the tracks they'd followed via coal oil lantern. They'd found tracks from a manufactured shoe, with the weight carried far forward, over the ball of the foot.

"We followed these tracks along the tree line, all the way up to the zoo. There must'a been a car, because we lost it right there. He stepped out of the damp grass and then just evaporated. We never saw him," York explained.

"A manufactured shoe and the weight carried way forward?" the Crimson Mask asked.

Garret nodded. "Yes as if the fellow had some sort of balance problem. I'd say he was fairly tall from the length of the strides, but considering we can't measure a shoe size, maybe he just lopes around like Schroeder over there."

Billy Schroeder only heard half of Garret's good-natured chiding. He saw something that didn't figure, just outside the harsh circle of light. He climbed out of the depression and circled toward the rear and a grizzled-looking black walnut tree. Leaning against the tree was a lever action repeating .22 caliber rifle. "Hey, Paulie, if you have a moment for police work, could you come over here and help me just a minute?"

Garret and York both went to where Schroeder stood. "What do you guys make of this?" York reached for the rifle, "I haven't seen one of these in a long time."

"Thoughts?" the Crimson Mask asked from below, and he pushed a wooden stake into the ground near an odd shaped track.

"What was he doing with a rifle in a public park?" York asked, followed by Garret's question, "What was his beef with these guys?"

"None of them were shot, as far as I can tell. They all have that same thin, deep gash one place or another," Edward Washa offered, which Phillip seconded with, "Why pose them up like this? Like he plays with them like they're dolls or statues."

"What I want to know is why a horse patrolman just happened to be riding by at dark in a park, miles off his beat?" Ted asked, and all five of the sergeants nodded or uttered their agreement.

"I think the killer is in a lot of pain. Something or a lot of somethings have caused him to have a break with reality. He is associating his actions with vindication," the Crimson Mask explained as they walked to the trucks.

Ted looked at the Sergeants. "Okay gentlemen who is waiting for the coroner?"

"Who's the coroner out here, anyway?" Garret asked.

"Doc Brascomb, Tracey Brascomb. They call him Butch, short for butcher. He's a drunk, but wouldn't you be if you had to do that all day?" Ed Washa said grimly.

"You have that many homicides out here?" York asked, his question getting the attention of Billy Schroeder.

"No, but the universities pay for cadavers and there's a brisk trade in unclaimed corpses. Doctor Brascomb is particularly talented in preserving them for study," Phillip explained. "He did the naked family for the State Fair. It was disgusting, and bizarre, and I couldn't stop looking at it."

"He is the best authority in the state when it comes to determining cause and manner of death. He and Derrick Merck wrote the best currently accepted criminal pathology textbook," Ted Warrick said, as if they should all have known.

The Crimson Mask offered. "Be vigilant gentlemen, I'm afraid there's more to this killer than crimes of passion. This fellow believes that he is performing a service for the public good. He will not see the error in his way and will likely be impossible to bring to justice. If we are lucky enough to catch him in the act at all, he will be prepared to fight to the death. We must keep this out of the papers for as long as possible."

Doc Clarke was asleep when footfalls on the front walk roused him, and then three steps up onto the porch brought him awake. Rapid-fire knocking on the door brought him from the bedroom, pistol in hand. He pulled back the curtain and then threw open the door.

"I got it. I think I know who, or what, is committing these murders!" Sandra Gray exclaimed as she stepped inside.

"What? Who?" Clarke asked as he hid the pistol.

"Think about it. All of these killings have been staged," she said quickly.

"Right, set up like a scene in a show, all but the one in Stooksbury Road, which was as I understand it a re-creation. What's on your mind?" Bob said as he shut the door.

"That's the point. They all re-create a tragedy that happened to someone else, because of an adverse relationship with another, usually unsavory character," she said with excitement.

"Right. The killer is setting these scenes up to shock the loved ones, because of some wrong they committed," he said nodding, but the scene tonight didn't fit.

"They're staged to add insult to injury, like the circus train!" She exclaimed. He tilted his head in confusion and she explained her epiphany in five points.

Doc Clarke and Dave Small were conducting inventory a week later than usual, due to the dictates of the Crimson Mask's recent late night escapades, either patrolling or lying in wait for the killer he'd dubbed Mr. Mnemonic, because he attacked his true victims by killing their loved ones in ghastly ways that would be nearly impossible to wipe from their minds.

Dave heard the honking bicycle horn and looked up. In the distance the sound of horns and a marching bass drum were barely audible. Then they both heard children running by on the sidewalk. They both stood up and sat their clipboards on the glass display case on the way to the door. The first of the circus wagon train was passing by as the two of them stepped out onto the sidewalk.

Scantly clothed acrobats did handstands and other feats on the backs of passing pachyderms. The clown fire brigade, marching band, and lion tamers passed by followed by the freak show wagon, drawn by the strong man. As it passed, Bob Clarke thought about his conversation with the lovely Sandra Gray.

The final vehicle in the circus wagon train was a festively painted white-panelled truck onto which a three dimensional riverscape had been painted with great attention to detail. On the river sailed a large wooden tub, crewed by a butcher, a baker, and a candlestick maker.

Doc Clarke ran into the drug store and shoved the door closed behind him with such gusto that the sign caught wind and turned itself to CLOSED. He rushed to the back room that served as the Crimson Mask's secret lab and he picked up one of the slips of paper that he'd found in Bronx Park. He turned around and was headed outside when he nearly ran headlong into Dave Small, who presented him with a small slip of heavy paper the size of a business card.

On one side was printed the image of a harlequin and a message which read, 'This is a free ticket. It is absolutely worthless. If presented the bearer will pay you two bits, in which case the free ticket will have been damaged and can be returned for a full refund.'

The other side of the ticket was a simple business card which advertised The Coney Island Carnival and Circus as the Most Spectacular Show on Earth. There was no contact information on the card. No name other than that of the circus. No address of the business office. No telephone number.

"Dave, I want you to follow that wagon train and see where it stops to set up. Keep your distance and if anyone takes notice get out of there," Doc ordered. The Mask's edge was in his voice. Dave nodded and slipped out the rear exit.

Doc Clarke eyed the card again and thought of Sandra. He walked over to the counter and picked up the telephone. He dialed the local exchange and waited.

The roadster rocketed through the gate at the Coney Island Fairgrounds and slid to a stop in front of the main building. The Crimson Mask leapt from his mount and drew his .38 automatic. He listened. Silence. A sign rattled on the gate. Someplace in the distance a dog was barking. He heard no sounds from within.

Sandra hadn't answered the phone at home, and she wasn't working or visiting her mother. Her schedule was regularly irregular, as was Dave's and his own. They'd planned it that way because of the nature of their relationships and the target they all wore, the price for their association with the Crimson Mask. He'd come here immediately assuming that The Coney Island Carnival would be at home if it was in town. He thought he was wrong, and based on first impressions it appeared to be so.

The Crimson Mask shot the lock off the hasp and kicked open the door. He ran inside the main building and found it eerily quiet. Odd shadows played on the walls via light emitted through holes in the roof. Something moved in his periphery and he turned quickly, aiming at the sound. Nothing.

He raced to a structure at the far end of the open space. As he neared the small office he had the feeling that he was being watched. He shouldered in the door and the sharp aroma of rodent droppings and stale urine assaulted his nose. He flipped the light switch and the bulb came on long enough to explode in a shower of sparks. When it did, no fewer than a dozen mice scattered. He bent to pick up a slip of paper and smiled. It was a tattered piece of notebook paper, on which was written in a very bold, childlike scrawl, 'Michael E. Minnick, a man who can memorize anything.'

"That's it!"

The tent crew had pitched the large circus tent and set the bleachers. They'd gotten everything ready for the show and gone home for the night. Tonight was rehearsal, tomorrow the Circus would open for three nights only. The spotlight was off when the masked men led the Dresden china beauty to the wheel and strapped her to it. She was not only blindfolded, but a gag kept her from making more than minimal sound.

The opening act was Two Gun Pete, the knife throwing sharpshooter. The Strongman and all the other members of the criminal menagerie were gathered in the front row to run through their acts before taking care of other business at the behest of the boss. On the far side of the arena, in the closest floor level seat to the exit, sat a dark and intense gentleman who wore a dark suit with a wide brimmed fedora, with a peculiar bash, worn low to hide his face. He raised his gaze when Two Gun Pete rode in on the back of a painted mare, the horse of a different color. The dark man's entire face was covered in hair, the same red-brown color that spilled over his collar.

The man on horseback rode into the center ring, guns blazing. Four cobalt blue jars were shattered by his bullets as he circled the ring on his first pass. The second pass was a victory ride, before his figure eight barrel run. When he returned to the starting marker, he spurred the horse and started the figure eight, shooting a melon off either side. At the top of the ark he pulled up sharply and reared the horse. He shot the red bull's-eye that controlled the wheel to which Sandra Gray had been strapped.

As the horse's front hooves returned to earth and the big animal rocketed forward, Pete saw the cops storming in the east and west entrances. He continued his routine, firing two more shots, exploding two more melons. At the bottom of the figure eight he leapt from the horse as a roadster raced into the arena.

The man driving the roadster wore a suit and a fedora, but Pete only saw the blood red mask. The car braked hard and slid sideways, and as it came to a stop the Crimson Mask leapt out. He broadcast a handful of small purplish stones. Pete threw four knives at Sandra, who spun on the wheel. Light glinted off the surface of the long, thin, razor-sharp knives as their promise of imminent death flew toward the target. The purple stones exploded with the sound of machine-gun fire causing the gunman and his horse to withdraw.

The Crimson Mask saw the suited man in the shadows across the arena as he leapt from the roadster. In his periphery he caught a flash of movement and the sparkle of light reflecting on polished steel. He glanced at the turning wheel and his hand went for the .38 automatic.

Four bullets left the bore of the Crimson Mask's pistol so fast that the muzzle emitted only a single pulsing flash. Three bullets hit their mark, tearing the knives off target, flying wildly away. The fourth bullet struck the flat pommel of the knife and caused it to tumble across its axis as well as spin. It continued on its trajectory, but instead of slicing into Sandra Gray's throat, the flat side slapped harmlessly against her shoulder and fell to the floor.

The Crimson Mask's feet touched the ground, and as he pivoted he was under fire. He cart-wheeled left and shoulder-rolled to the right. Hoof beats thundered away and the sounds of angry cops rose as they flooded in to subdue the no longer peaceful spectators.

Thirteen arrests were made that night, but the man who watched from the shadows, Michael E. Minnick, also known as Mr. Mnemonic, had vanished in the ensuing chaos. The bizarre murders in the Five Boroughs ceased. While each member of the criminal menagerie was guilty in some form, the mastermind was still out there. The Crimson Mask had only uncovered a worldwide cabal of evil. While the deviant are still at work, fear not, for the Crimson Mask is at work to make criminals pay for their misdeeds.

THE END

Writing the Crimson Mask

The opportunity to write a Crimson Mask story was something that I happened upon accidentally, as I have generally happened upon most of the best writing opportunities I've been fortunate enough to get. The character of Bob Clarke and his alter-ego, the Crimson Mask, are very relatable to me and probably a lot of other writers who have grown up in the comic book age. The idea of an average guy with an angry dark side who does good by harming those who generally can't complain, a.k.a. the vigilante, is an appealing project because of all of the conventions that go out the window when you write a smart and motivated character that best operates in the grey space between the law and the lawless.

This is a first for me and I've never written on any project relating to any classic pulp characters. I guess it's a matter of due respect to those who paved the way, but this effort will be telling of whether I am equal to the task. As someone totally unfamiliar with the Crimson Mask, I simply hoped to do justice to the original. As a person who oft suffers my own ego, I humbly hope that I have done justice to Norm Daniels and the other authors who were Frank Johnson.

Upon reading a couple of Crimson Mask tales I decided that any involvement I had in writing the character might be best served by giving him an archenemy to deal with. As with all bigger-than-life characters, the Crimson Mask has had a seminal tragedy which has driven him to find a means toward a very bitter end. I think Michael E. Minnick (Mr. Mnemonic) is a villain who fills the requirement for a despicable villain with whom everyone can sympathize and despise because he is, in his outwardly actions, the retribution that anyone who has ever been held accountable for being different has wanted to exact. He arrives with an elusive appearance behind the scenes to set the stage for a further involvement, and shows his willingness to sacrifice those who do his bidding to make his own escape.

I hope that through my challenge of trying to find a classic voice for what I hope will be many tales of the Crimson Mask—learning who my characters are, and what they want to say—I have written you some meaty sustenance for that dark thing that dwells within, craving always the next story. Happy reading!

J. WALT LAYNE lives in Springfield, Ohio. He is a veteran of the US Army, a married father of three and a voracious reader and prolific writer. He is the author of *Frank Testimony,* a legal thriller set in Bedford, Mississippi in the 1950s. He is also the author and creator of The Champion City Series of pulp detective stories to be published exclusively by Pro Se Press (March 2013). He has written a laundry list of articles for Backwoodsman Magazine and is the Op-Ed columnist for The Albany Journal (Albany, Georgia). You can catch up with him on Facebook as Author J Walt Layne.

LOVE THOSE B HEROES

From day one we at Airship 27 Productions set out not only to help keep pulps alive via our new anthologies and novels, but we also had a second objective; to put the spotlight squarely on the lesser known pulp B characters who were mostly forgotten by today's fans. Talk pulps with most genre fans and you will constantly hear about the Shadow, Doc Savage or the Spider. Bring up characters like the Avenger, Secret Agent X or Domino Lady and people start to look at you as if you are speaking a foreign language.

Which is why, in the past eight years (going on nine) we've been thrilled to bring you new adventures of those characters and others like Jim Anthony Super Detective, the Moon Man and Ravenwood: Stepson of Mystery. Now, with this volume, we are thrilled to add the Crimson Mask to our line-up.

THE CRIMSON MASK

"Detective Novels" presented every other month an extraordinary crime fighter, the Crimson Mask. The author was Norm Daniels writing as Frank Johnson and there were fifteen stories between 1940 and 1944.

Doctor Robert "Bob" Clarke, Ph.G. at 28 was young strong, kindly face with keen eyes and a very athletic build. Good looking, vigorous, plus being a rather commanding figure, he was a graduate pharmacist, druggist, and had completed those courses on funds left by his father, a former police sergeant, killed in the line of duty by gangsters. Bullets were fired in the back of the officer's head. As he lay dying, there occurred a strange rush of blood to his face which formed a macabre mask, *a crimson mask!* Upon seeing it, Bob Clarke became inspired to become his father's avenger, the Crimson Mask.

The Crimson Mask wore a black suit, dark tie, crepe-soled shoes, and a red velvet domino mask. He carried a .38 automatic.

As Doc Clarke he owned a drug store which dispensed drugs and medical supplies only. He also worked in the pharmaceutical laboratories of City Hospital. He was well versed in Scientific Criminology, Ballistics,

Toxicology, Chemistry and Metallurgy. Clarke could throw his voice like a ventriloquist, studied safe-cracking, knew body nerve centers, had a very keen analytical mind and carefully cultivated his own powers of observation.

As the Crimson Mask, he took bizarre cases, complex mysteries that puzzled the police and taxed the ingenuity of both himself and the police. He was a near legendary figure who appeared whenever some weird or ominous crime had taken place. Like the cops, the underworld did not know what to make of him and considered him a foe to be eliminated at any cost.

He was aided by a trio of brave souls: **Theodore Warrick,** 60, grey-haired and former Police Commissioner of the city in which he operated. **David Small,** a former college roommate, short of stature and somewhat rotund, fair-haired, healthy pink cheeks, came from a wealthy family, worked at the City Hospital Research Lab. He would manage the drug store whenever Clarke was off on a Crimson Mask affair. **Sandra Gray** was a stunning young woman, 5'3", with a smooth creamy complexion, full, beautifully curved lips and cool grey eyes. Known as Sandy, she worked as a Nurse's Aide in City Hospital. She could handle a gun and was a skilled driver.

The drug store was located in lower Manhattan, three blocks from the East River. The address: Corner of East Avenue and Carmody Street. The building stood on a dimly-lit corner. The entire neighborhood was devoted to the young druggist and affectionately called him Doc Clarke. Beneath the back counter where he worked, Clarke had installed a special red light that was connected to Commissioner Warrick's home. When it flashed red that was the signal the Crimson Mask was needed.

In the grand tradition of most masked avengers, Clarke loved Sandy and knew she wanted nothing more than to marry and raise a family. But he was obsessed with his war on crime in the memory of his slain father. Because of her love, she was willing to wait until the day the Crimson Mask retired.

And there you have it, the history of the Crimson Mask. Now, thanks to the wonderful imaginations of J. Walt Layne, Terrence McCauley, C. William Russette and Gary Lovisi, he and his allies are back, once again waging their endless battle against big-city villainy. We think you are going to love these new adventures wonderfully illustrated by artist Andy Fish who also provided our stunning cover.

We at Airship 27 Productions are thrilled with this book and are most anxious to hear your thoughts on it. We welcome your letters. Until then, thanks as ever for your continued support.

Ron Fortier
9/6/2013
Fort Collins, CO
(www.Airship27.com)
(Airship27@comcast.net)

Airship
27

JIM ANTHONY
SUPER-DETECTIVE

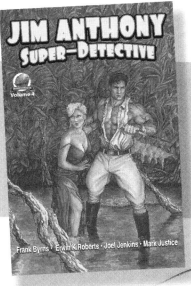

He's half Comanche, half Irish and ALL AMERICAN!! Jim Anthony the Super Detective returns in his fourth volume of brand new adventures from Airship 27 Productions.

Traveling the globe, Anthony battles all manner of twisted villainy in four new tales and his challenges are herculean. Writers Erwin K. Roberts, Joel Jenkins, Frank Byrns and Mark Justice have whipped up a quartet of high adventure stories that are the hallmark of the Super Detective. From Mexico, where he encounters a Nazi spy ring to the streets of Manhattan where he hunts down a brutal serial killer, Jim Anthony proves once again why he is one of the most exciting and fun heroes ever created in the golden age of American pulps.

This volume, the fourth in an on-going series, features interior illustrations by Michael Neno and a dazzling cover by Eric Meador, with book designs by Rob Davis. Airship 27 Productions is thrilled to continue the exploits of the one and only, Jim Anthony – Super Detective.

PULP FICTION FOR A NEW GENERATION!

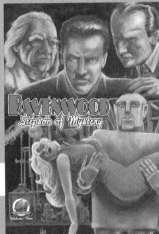

Made in the USA
Charleston, SC
29 October 2013